FROM A SHOCKING PHALLIC RITUAL
ON THE AFRICAN COAST . . .
TO STEAMY SLAVELOVE
IN A NEW ORLEANS BROTHEL . . .
TO A SEETHING SLAVE REBELLION
IN A CARIBBEAN PRISON-FORTRESS . . .

DRAGONARD RISING continues the story of the
powerful and enigmatic Richard Abdee, once a public
whipmaster, now sire to a tormented dynasty of
mixed blood . . . a man whose perverse passions and
wanton lusts have made him the most feared slave-
master of the New World.

DRAGONARD RISING

An explosive saga of slavery and sin.

GOLDEN APPLE BOOKS by Rupert Gilchrist

DRAGONARD
THE MASTER OF DRAGONARD HILL
DRAGONARD BLOOD
DRAGONARD RISING
THE SIEGE OF DRAGONARD HILL

Dragonard Rising

RUPERT GILCHRIST

GOLDEN APPLE PUBLISHERS

DRAGONARD RISING

A Golden Apple Publication / December 1984

Golden Apple is a trademark of Golden Apple Publishers

CONTENTS

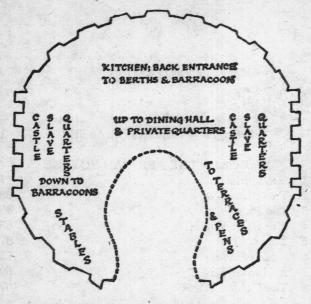

KITCHEN; BACK ENTRANCE
TO BERTHS & BARRACOON

UP TO DINING HALL
& PRIVATE QUARTERS

CASTLE SLAVE QUARTERS

CASTLE SLAVE QUARTERS

DOWN TO
BARRACOONS

STABLES

TO TERRACES
& PENS

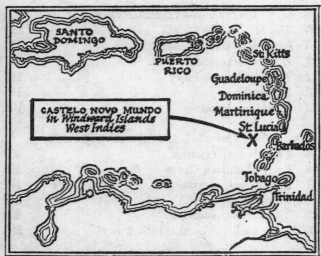

SANTO
DOMINGO

PUERTO
RICO

St Kitts

Guadeloupe

Dominica

Martinique

St. Lucia

CASTELO NOVO MUNDO
in Windward Islands
West Indies

X

Barbados

Tobago

Trinidad

Prologue

FANTASY MASTER

Castelo Novo Mundo
Windward Islands, West Indies
1803

Few things in life impressed thirty-four-year-old Anna Tyler any more but the first glimpse of *Castelo Novo Mundo* towering like a spectre above the mottled blue water of the Caribbean left her breathless. She had not beheld such a threatening—yet tantalizing—sight since the first time she had seen a Negro buck stripped naked in an auction house, and that had been some ten, twelve years ago now.

Standing beside her husband this afternoon on the foredeck of their brigantine, the *Southern Zephyr*, Anna Tyler gazed spellbound at the castle's black walls rising from the utmost perimeter of a miniscule island of solid rock, the waves licking over the lichen-covered base, ebbing against the indeterminate seam where the hewn stones joined the craggy bedrock.

The only entrance into the waveswept castle was through an arched gate, an iron bossed portcullis raised by grinding chains, giving way to a small but deep harbor where the *Southern Zephyr* soon weighed anchor, an enclosed port edged by a sloping dirt yard from which a myriad of doors and posterns opened onto stairways and trails leading to the many sections of the castle.

This trip to the West Indies had been Anna's

brainchild. She and her husband, Hugh Tyler, owned an auction house on Duvall Street in New Orleans. Having heard from one of her waterfront spies that an Englishman, Richard Abdee, was bringing a new cargo of prisoners from Africa to this isolated fortress in the Windward Islands, Anna had immediately recognized the advantages of buying slaves when they were unloaded fresh from the Atlantic voyage, bidding on them before they were shipped on to established markets. She knew that, apart from owning this slave station in the Caribbean, Richard Abdee had a reputation for choosing blacks as adeptly as most men chose their linen handkerchiefs. She urged Hugh to chance the voyage here. Her first surprise was to find that Abdee had not yet returned from Africa with the slave cargo.

The initial days at *Castelo Novo Mundo* passed quickly for Anna Tyler, the servants extending every hospitality to the Tylers, a treatment which Anna interpreted as being only natural and due to wealthy white people. She roamed through cavernous rooms and echoing halls, closely examining everything she saw.

Hugh Tyler spent less time than his wife studying furniture, tapestries, and sprawling oil portraits of swarthy noblemen dressed in pleated ruffs, interesting himself instead with the young black wenches who served as waiting girls. Anna gladly let him pursue his veneries, his absence giving her more time to explore . . . and think.

On the tenth day, Abdee still had not arrived from Africa but, by this time, Anna was busily questioning the small staff of resident slaves. She learned that Portuguese grandees had built this fortress two hundred years ago as protection against buccaneers. When Portugal's holdings in the West Indies began to dwindle, though, and they lost colonial power in the Caribbean, the grandees finally abandoned this once fabled stronghold in the New World which they had proudly named *Castelo Novo Mundo*.

In her quest for information about its present owner, Anna interrogated the cook, the serving wenches, even the gardeners for any bits of personal information about Richard Abdee, only becoming frustrated when they refused to discuss their master intimately with a stranger. Also, there were certain sections of the castle they would not allow her to enter.

Anna caught glimpses of Abdee's genius for organization. He stored a bountiful supply of food and fresh water. She saw small yards where poultry, livestock, swine were kept in neatly latticed coops, pens and sties. There were hidden terraces within the castle where garden plots were planted with vegetables, fruit, and berries, tended daily by chattering black women and bashful picaninnies. Dungeons also existed deep within the castle, a musty zone laying far below the lapping water line of the Caribbean, sunk beneath the more airy quarters where the sailors were assigned.

Gradually, Anna Tyler was beginning to interpret the very sight of *Castelo Novo Mundo*—rising aloof, mysterious, strong—as the very essence of what she imagined Richard Abdee to be himself. His headquarters were solid and weatherbeaten on the exterior, yet, within, the workings were complex, intricate, and above all, abounding with every form of sexuality. She knew about this sexuality from her husband's behavior: Hugh seemed content spending his nights in a bedroom on a lower floor.

But Anna Tyler still had not discovered how the Englishman, Richard Abdee, had come to control this impregnable rock, nor the reason why he had left his previous home in the West Indies—the fabled Dragonard Plantation on the leeward island of St. Kitts—and come here to live in near isolation.

Those were only two of the many questions which she planned to ask Magnus tonight—the ebullient young black man whom Abdee had given the title of "overseer," the person who was Anna's last hope for information, and perhaps the first male to give her a sampling of the castle's sexuality.

* * *

Pacing restlessly across the Aubusson carpet in her bedroom at *Castelo Novo Mundo,* Anna wondered if she had acted wisely by inviting Magnus to visit her at such a late hour. What if he became violent when he realized the true nature of her invitation? That she was more interested in learning secrets about his English master than spending the night making love with a `. . . nigger?

Stopping in front of a cheval mirror in one corner of the high-ceilinged room, Anna surveyed her trim figure in the smoky glass. She saw that the bodice of her claret silk gown was cut daringly low. That her auburn hair glistened in the soft glow from the beeswax candles flickering on ormolu wall scounces. That the diamond necklace delicately complimented her creamy skin.

Next, she caught the reflections in the mirror of the rich furnishing behind her in the bedroom—the ornately carved bed, the Flemish wall tapestries, gilt chairs, cabriolet-legged tables. She smiled as she thought how these lavish appointments belied the castle's purpose, that it served as a way station in the Caribbean for running slaves from Africa to the New World.

Momentarily forgetting about her appearance, and the effect she hoped to have on Magnus, Anna's business mind began to work. She thought of the two other merchants who had only arrived today at the castle, Claude Saint-Barbot coming from Martinique and Ignatio Soto from Cuba. Their appearance here at first had angered her but, the more she thought about them, the more she realized that her original idea had been correct. That slave markets everywhere were starving for African flesh and brawn. She would rather compete here than in New Orleans.

Suddenly hearing a knock on the bedroom door, Anna quickly glanced back to the cheval mirror, pulling the bodice further down her ivory cleavage, taking one last appraisal of her slim face in the flickering candlelight.

Anna Tyler was always honest with herself. She knew that she was not a devastating beauty, nor as young as the creamy-brown wenches with whom her husband was wasting his time again tonight—and every night since their arrival here.

Nevertheless, Anna Tyler had a quality which few other females—white or black, youthful or mature—enjoyed. She was shrewd. She was a business woman. She knew how to get what she wanted in the world. She knew when to trade, what to barter, how to push. She was, in fact, pleased that Hugh was not troubling her. The freedom gave her more time to do things her way. And tonight she was willing to go to any extremes—even to submit her body to a black slave—in exchange for information about the man who had come to feed her fantasies of power in the last ten days—Richard Abdee.

*   *   *

7

Magnus lay naked beside Anna on the four-poster bed. He propped the side of his shaven head on one large hand and toyed with a ringlet of Anna's auburn hair while he smiled at her laying rigidly on the bed. Anna was angry now, staring petulantly up at the pleated canopy. Her plans seemed to be going awry.

In a deep-chested but gentle voice, Magnus said, "I thought you wasn't worried about your husband, Missus."

She snapped, "Who says I'm worried about my husband?" His confidence annoyed her. She had expected him to be like the black men back in Louisiana, to feel wary of a white lady's interest in him, to act more deferential. She wondered what Richard Abdee did to his black people to make them behave in such a self-assured manner. Didn't this nigger know that it was a privilege even to *talk* to a white lady? Here he was playing with her hair, running his hands idly over her body, asking her personal questions as if they were established lovers!

Smoothing the pink underside of his brown thumb down her pert chin, Magnus asked playfully, "What's you thinking about then? Where's your thoughts?"

The directness of the question, the touch of his hand so near her throat, his inquisitive stares irritated her. She pulled away from him, blurting, "Your master must be very free with you!"

Laying back in the softness of the feather mattress, Magnus crossed his muscled arms, and allowed his naked masculinity to jut in near hardness over the bulky brown bag of his scrotum. He said, "Lots of folks talk about the freedom Master Abdee gives us here. But you'll get used to it, Missus. All you got to do is pretend us niggers are . . . people." Chuckling,

8

he looked down at his broad feet as he twitched his big toe.

Anna definitely did not like the irony in his voice. He sounded too informed. Even educated. Everybody knew that an educated nigger was a trouble maker. And why was he acting so relaxed? Not acting more grateful?

She said disdainfully, "And when do I get the honor of meeting this considerate master of yours, boy?"

"Hells, woman. You can't rush no trip to Africa. Master Abdee, he never knows how long it takes him to get back from Africa. First, he's got to buy those bush niggers. Then he's got to gets them loaded. There's the crossing back home. . . . No, you can't count that trip in days. You got to take weather into consideration. You got to figure on maybe trouble with the crew. Or flux breaking out. A few niggers maybe escaping from their chains."

Magnus was leaning on his arm again, surveying Anna's trim body now half-covered by the linen counterpane, the lace borders secreting the pinkness of her nipples.

Anna said loftily, "Mister Abdee must also take into account a few things himself. I haven't travelled all the way from New Orleans to sit all night in this room! Nor spend the day walking up and down, up and down that filthy harbor yard out there, watching wretched picaninnies chasing each other like mongrel dogs! This place is like a . . . prison!"

"Master Abdee, he don't send you no hand written invitation to come here, Missus. Not to my knowledge, anyway. We lets you in here like we lets in that Cuban and the dandy from Martinique. Because Master Abdee's talked a lot about you. But you ain't the first nigger dealers to come here. And you won't be the last." Reaching forward, Magnus petted her bare shoulder, adding more softly, "But, Missus, maybe you're one of the prettiest. . . ."

Brushing his hand away, she said, "Don't be so familiar!"

"Familiar? Hells, Missus. You're the one who invited me to come up here tonight."

"Don't be impudent with me . . . slave!"

"'Slave' is it?" Magnus asked, pulling back and eyeing her, the smile disappearing from his broad face. "Sure, I'm a slave, Missus. But I ain't *your* slave. I belong to Master Abdee. I'm mighty proud of that fact, too. All of us niggers here are proud of the man who owns us."

Moving towards the edge of the bed, Magnus began to change his mind about pleasuring himself with this Louisiana white woman. True, he had been anxious to make love to her. She had the kind of trim body he remembered ogling as a young boy. Since Abdee had purchased him in New Orleans five years ago, brought him here and made him overseer because of his ability to read and write, Magnus had seen very few white-skinned women. He still wanted to fulfill his boyhood dreams of making love to one of those fair-skinned, slim-hipped Louisiana ladies. But Magnus wanted to do it his way. He wanted the act to be reciprocal. He wanted to make love with Anna Tyler like he did with the black girls. He wanted her to love him, too. He thought that maybe this was not the right Louisiana lady for him after all.

Reaching for his iron-hard bicep, Anna pulled him back towards her and spoke in a more friendly, less aggressive tone. She began, "Tell me about this . . . master of yours."

Magnus shook his head in bewilderment. "I just

can't figures you out, white woman. First, you whispers to me down in the yard to come up to your room and visit you tonight. I gets here. You act all sweet. You runs your hands all over me as soon as I gets in that door there. You holds your little pink mouth up to me for some kisses. You fights me a little when I try to rush towards this here fancy bed. You don't fights me hard. Just fights me enough to tell a nigger boy you ain't no common pecker-hungry slut. But when we strips off our clothes and lays here naked, you gets all cold. You calls me names. You calls me 'boy' and 'slave.' I thinks then maybe I have no business here at all. I decides on leaving. But when I starts to go, you gets all sweet-talking again. What you really wants from me, white lady? You wants loving or you wants to go on acting slave boss?"

Under any other circumstance, Anna Tyler would not listen to talk like this from a black person. She would ordinarily rebuke any slave who spoke to her in such a disrespectful manner. Unfortunately, she had not even begun to pick his brain. She still had facts to glean about Richard Abdee.

Pursuing her more feminine, helpless attack, she suppressed her fury and continued in a halting voice, "You must not be angry . . . Magnus. I am very . . . nervous. I'm not myself tonight. I feel like such a . . . stranger here. My husband is never with me . . ."

Stopping, she wistfully shook her head, confessing, "The fact is I'm lonely. The only thing to distract me from loneliness is this castle. I've seen so little of it really, but . . ."

Magnus interrupted with a firm voice, "You can't see no more of this place than whats we lets you see, Missus. Mister Abdee, he don't take kindly to folks poking around this big, old place of his."

11

"Abdee! That's all I hear! Abdee! I've heard so many stories about him. Strange, contradictory stories. How he runs this castle. Why he lives here. How he once owned a plantation on the English island of St. Kitts . . ."

Nodding, Magnus said, "That be Dragonard Plantation."

"And 'Dragonard'? Wasn't 'Dragonard' the name for a public whipmaster on one of the English islands? Wasn't Richard Abdee the 'Dragonard' for the English government on the island of . . . St. Kitts?"

Magnus confirmed, "He lived on the island of St. Kitts before coming here. He had Dragonard Plantation there."

"Then he must have named his plantation after his public post of whipmaster . . . the Dragonard," Anna said, considering the words as she spoke them.

Piqued by the perversity of Abdee naming a plantation after a contemptible position in the community, she proceeded more excitedly, "I also heard that a slave uprising destroyed Dragonard Plantation. Is that correct? That Abdee lost everything he owned on St. Kitts? That all his slaves were sold to America or escaped to other islands?" Letting one finger now gently trace the muscle on Magnus's upper arm, she asked, "Is that all true, Magnus?"

"What's true and what's lies ain't no business of mine to tell."

"But how did Abdee make the enormous step from being 'Dragonard' to owning a vast plantation? And where's his family? Doesn't he have a wife? Children? Heirs? What's happened to *them*?"

"He's got a few half-caste suckers running around this place here. That's all the family I knows about. But those are just picaninnies from his wenches here."

12

"What does he do with his time here? He surely doesn't spend all his time siring babies! He must go crazy with no companionship except . . ." She quickly stopped herself.

Looking at her, Magnus finished the sentence. "With no companions except us *niggers?*"

Anna shrugged. Why should she deny that "nigger" was the word she was going to say? She had no reason to respect the feelings of black people.

Sitting on the edge of the four-poster bed, Magnus spoke in a solemn voice. "Master Abdee's happy living here with us black folks, Missus. He's got all he wants. If he do got kin someplace in the world, let's just say he's turned his back on them. His kin now is us slaves. Us slaves he calls his 'people.' He don't sell none of his 'people.' We're his help. His friends. He's got here all the wenches he needs for loving. He's got those two pretty maids, Eula and Daisy, who you husband is always chasing. He's got that short wench with a whip, Luma, who the Cuban has been trying to get today. He's got wenches you ain't even seen yet. Gals working in the weaving rooms, the gardens, the storehouses. Even Consuela, the chubby cook you see down in the kitchen, she's all juicy for him."

Stopping, studying Anna Tyler as she tried to cover herself with the lace-edged counterpane, Magnus said, "Now, is we going to keep on talking? Because if we is, I'm going to pull on my togs and get out of here. I ain't risking my black skin in bed with a white woman just for some talk!"

Anna heaved her breasts with a nervous sigh. The time had come. She would have to make love with this head-strong nigger or take a chance on him never talking to her again. He could become her one ally here if . . .

13

She held one hand out to him, saying as she closed her eyes, "You will be gentle with me, won't you Magnus?"

"Gentle?" he repeated, falling on top of her and scooping her small ivory body in his bulging brown arms, "I'll be so gentle with you, Missus . . ."

Magnus fought himself from ramming the crown of his taut penis immediately into the soft brown hair between her legs. Covering her neck with kisses, working his quickly darting tongue down her breasts, teasing each nipple with a playful bite, he slowly felt her body responding beneath him.

Soon, Anna wrapped her arms around the broadness of his back, thrusting her groin upwards to accept the first few inches of what seemed to her a terrifying sized, almost animal-like, penis. She was thinking again how she would work the conversation back to Richard Abdee after Magnus had reached his climax when—suddenly—she felt him prodding deeper inside her, his negroid thickness successfully coaxing her femininity to accommodate him, his hands gently working her breasts into a sensitivity totally new to her. She tried to conquer her growing response to Magnus, but the warmth of his mouth against her lips made her momentarily forget all plans. She sunk deeper into the feather mattress, thinking about the tower rising from the Caribbean, trying to conjure up a picture of Richard Abdee, remembering that a black man was now making love to her, then thinking yet again of this castellated tower, *Castelo Novo Mundo.*

14

Book One
THE AFRICAN VOYAGE

I

"STORE MAN"

A line of tumbledown huts and a dilapidated stockade made from palm trunks were the remnants of Port Weston's more prosperous days on the African Slave Coast. Tom Weston still flew the British colors from a pole standing askew on the driftwood littered beach but the red-white-and-blue flag was slowly becoming bleached and ripped by sun, rain, and torrential rains.

Tom Weston no longer was an offical government factor. He had lost his charter by buying contraband slaves from Spanish privateers and reselling them to British merchants. Too proud to return to England a ruined man, Weston remained a prisoner of the Slave Coast, an Englishman with nothing to look forward to except the stifling heat, aching loneliness and, most probably, a convulsing death from yellow fever . . . if syphilis did not come first, gnawing away at his brain.

Richard Abdee liked to do business with disillusioned men like Tom Weston. They did not interfere in his dealings with the black slave dealers who brought captives from the mountainous inlands of Africa. A keg of rum could ensure Weston's cooperation and, today, he lay drunk in one of the palm branch huts while Abdee bargained on the beach with a slave dealer, one of the many African merchants called "caboceers" plying their trade in human lives along the Slave, Guinea, and Gold Coasts of Western Africa.

Looking overhead at the tattered Union Jack now beginning to flutter on its rope, Abdee felt relieved that he had purchased—and loaded—the majority of his cargo. A wind was building. He could soon return to his ship anchored in the mouth of the cove. He would be sailing by midday for *Castelo Novo Mundo*.

Abdee's ony disappointment was that this morning's caboceer had not brought as many Negroes to Port Weston as he had anticipated. Abdee would sail westward with a profitable load of slaves but not the brimming cargo which he had hoped to buy.

Settling his sombre blue eyes on the gaunt caboceer known as "Store Man," Abdee listened as the Negro praised the coffle of chained prisoners stretching across the sand behind him, a line of tired and half-naked Africans extending across the width of the beach to a tangled palm forest.

"Store Man" wore a black tricorne hat; a white robe hung in rumpled folds from his bony frame; ropes of cowrie shells encircled his scrawny neck to denote his wealth. Digging his bare toes into the wet sand like fleshy talons, "Store Man" pointed a burled staff toward the line of shackled Negroes and explained in pidgin English that the captives were from the Ashanti tribe beyond the Volta River. That he and his guards had traveled on foot and in canoes for six days to bring them to Abdee at Port Weston.

Abdee stood listening with his hands tucked into the waistband of his doeskin breeches, his weight resting on one booted foot. He respected this black man negotiating the sale of Negroes into slavery as he would respect a white man selling his own people: slavery was an enterprise from which any keen-eyed person could profit. Abdee credited "Store Man" as being one of the shrewdest caboceers on the Slave Coast. He dreaded the time when "Store Man" would learn the true value of his human merchandise, when the price for Negroes would rise here and markedly effect the white men's profits.

The caboceer proudly thumbed his sunken chest, bragging, " 'Store Man' gets best prisoners from Ibo Tribe. Chief Zomo gives 'Store Man' best war prisoners to sell for him. All strong men and ripe women like these. You look now." He tugged at the sleeve of Abdee's nankeen shirt to study his prisoners.

Abdee could already see that these Ashantis were rugged, healthy people. This only increased his disappointment that "Store Man" had not brought him more than fifty prisoners. He had expected three times this amount of Ashanti prisoners captured by the war-loving Ibo Tribe.

He asked, "Why do you not bring more people? Why does 'Store Man' not keep the promise he made to me the last time I was here?"

"You buy these now. We make good agreement. You take today's prisoners away in great boat." "Store Man" pointed his staff toward Abdee's ship.

The hold of the *Petit Jour* was already packed with more than four hundred slaves, people mostly from the district of Dinkara and the foothills of Anase. Abdee knew that these Ashantis were a sound investment, the members of that noble tribe always fetching high prices in West Indian and North American auction houses. "Store Man" had again brought him men with well-muscled arms, women with sturdy legs, children that promised a healthy maturity.

Nevertheless, having fitted the hold of the *Petit Jour* to carry six hundred slaves across the Atlantic, Abdee had hoped to fill every space on the wooden shelves. Unlike "Store Man," Abdee knew the fortunes now being paid in the Americas and the Caribbeans for prime-class slaves.

Pausing in front of a tall Negress wearing a width of coarse weave around her fulsome body, "Store Man" said anxiously, "Look here. See young wife of Ashanti king killed in battle. Look here. She his kinga. Strong woman from good *bogna*. Look here," he insisted, reaching toward the Negress's breast to rip away the tattered covering. "This woman kinga."

Folding one arm across his chest, Abdee rubbed the golden stubble on his square jaw as he studied the naked woman. She was tall standing, only a few inches shorter than himself. Her black hair was intricately plaited against a well-shaped skull. A wooden collar was locked around her long neck, iron chains connecting the rings to similar collars on prisoners in front and back of her. The woman's hands were bound with leather thongs. Iron manacles restricted her bare feet.

Scrutinizing the curve of her ebony-colored breasts, the sinewy blackness of her nipples, a slim waist spreading to voluptuous hips and high-placed buttocks, Abdee nodded his head with approval. He slowly repeated the pidgin word which "Store Man" had used to describe this Negress's position in her tribe . . .

". . . 'kinga'." That could be her new name. *Kinga*.

Like the male warriors in the slave coffle, the

black woman squared her naked shoulders. She continued to stare coldly at the back of the man in front of her. She stood proudly in her nakedness as if she wore the finest feather and shell-beaded *batakari* cape of the Ashanti Tribe.

"Store Man" grinned at Abdee's immediate fascination with the Negress. He urged, "Feel this kinga! Feel her take white man good!" He grabbed Abdee's hand and pushed it toward the patch of wiry black hair between her legs.

Abdee pulled to free his hand from "Store Man's" grip but, when he saw that the Ashanti woman remained immobile, he stepped closer. He slowly extended his middle finger and positioned it toward the patch between her legs.

The pubic hairs glistened with perspiration. The vaginal lips were moist. Abdee pushed his finger deeper into the wool. He felt a warmth. Next, he curled his middle finger and began to probe more deeply, to work for the liquid softness he enjoyed to feel inside a woman.

Suddenly, he felt a quick tightening as if his finger had been clamped by an iron vice. His finger turned numb. He quickly pulled away his hand and cursed.

"Store Man" laughed, beating his staff on the soggy beach in glee when he saw the surprise expression on Abdee's face. He said, "Woman trick! Ashanti woman knows good trick! Yes, Abdee? Good trick?" "Store Man" turned to show him the remainder of his prisoners, still chuckling at Abdee's surprise.

Remaining where he was, Abdee stared in disbelief at the tall Ashanti woman. His middle finger still tingled from the sudden contraction of her vagina. He had never before felt such control of female muscle and tissue. He knew from the Negress's impassive face that she had not acted as many Negresses might have done—to impress a potential buyer with her unique qualities. That she had done it to defy him. Abdee decided at that moment that he would not sell this Ashanti woman whom "Store Man" called "Kinga." He would keep her as one of his special people at *Castelo Novo Mundo*.

*   *   *

Preceeding down the line of prisoners, Abdee prodded the hard biceps of men who would fetch high prices as laborers on the sugar *plats* of the West Indies. He spotted more than a dozen boys who could be trained as stable hands on Cuban *fincas*. There were many shapely youngsters of both sexes who could quickly develop into fine domestic servants in the neo-classical manor houses of the American South. He noticed many wide-hipped wenches who were good prospects for breeding farms. Yet no one among the remaining prisoners had the noble stance of Kinga. She was undoubtedly a black aristocrat, one of the Africans whom Abdee knew the Ashantis call *bakomba*.

Abdee finally saw a man toward the end of the coffle who did not please him. He reached forward and grabbed the sullen man's chin, studying the garish lines and curlicues of pinpoints marking his prune black face, excessive gashes decorating his sinewy shoulders.

Shaking his head disapprovingly, Abdee said, "No, 'Store Man.' Not this one. Markings like these frighten white men. A planter will not buy a slave like this. Take him from the coffle." He glanced down at the few remaining Negroes in the line to spot any more disfigured faces or decorative blemishes.

Grabbing for Abdee's arm, "Store Man" argued, "This good nigger. He smart nigger."

Abdee pulled away his hand from "Store Man's" grip. He did not want to feel any surprises which this male could perform for him; he was not interested in an oversized penis or the smoothness of a man's anus. He did not want to hear any spiel from "Store man" about this slave glowering beneath his excessive tribal markings.

He said flatly, "I do not want any like him in the next coffle. You understand that? No more tattooed Africans."

"This nigger good," "Store Man" insisted. "This nigger smart. He called 'Pra.' Pra has magic in his hands. Pra puts marks on tribesmen faces. He pierces ears with sharp antelope bone. He stretches lips with wood. Pra smart nigger. Good slave Pra makes. Good nigger slave for white man."

Abdee argued, "Men in New World do not want blacks who decorate their faces and bodies. We do not pierce ears with bone and wire. White masters do not like slaves stretching their lips big with wood."

"You listen to 'Store Man', Abdee. You listen. I give Abdee this Pra nigger. I give Pra to Abdee for gift. You take him away on great boat. You see him work good in New World. Pra good. You buy more next time. You see."

Eyeing "Store Man's" stubborn face, Abdee asked suspiciously, "Tell me about the next tribe Chief Zomo battles. Do they stretch their lips with wood? Gash their skin with bone? Will there be more men like this?" He motioned toward the Ashanti craftsman, Pra.

"Store Man" avoided Abdee's searching blue eyes, answering, "No, no, you take this nigger. You try. You

23

do not like nigger I bring no more to Port Weston. You take him. I give gift to Abdee."

Knowing that he could not offend "Store Man" by refusing this offer of a gift, Abdee cursed the clever trader under his breath for trapping him into accepting Pra.

Turning from the slave coffle, Abdee trudged across the beach toward a palm hut, saying "I'll take your gift. But I will not buy more men with gashes on their bodies. I will leave them behind in Port Weston to starve. I will give you nothing for them, 'Store Man.' Nothing."

Running after Abdee, "Store man" puffed, "What you bring today?"

Abdee looked toward the strident sound of a Mynah calling from the palm forest, answering disinterestedly, "Sabres. Iron pots. Necklaces red and yellow like fire. And—" rubbing his thumb and forefinger together, he said, "—I brought the cloth you asked me to bring. I brought the cloth as thin as water. I brought you . . . silk."

"Store Man" pushed back the tricorne on his head with a crooked forefinger, gasping, "You brought . . . silk?"

Continuing toward the hut, Abdee said, "I have been saving the silk only for you, 'Store Man.' Many caboceers have asked for silk. Good caboceers who bring me many slaves. But I told them that the cloth as thin as water is for my good friend from the Ibo Tribe. I told them that "Store Man" is bringing me all the prisoners I want. But then when you come to Port Weston, I see nothing. Only a few prisoners for me to take away to the New World."

"Next time," "Store man" said eagerly, digging his staff into the beach as he ran along side Abdee, tossing flecks of sand behind him with each dig, his bare feet treading over shells and remnants of small, withered sand crabs.

"When is 'next time'?" Abdee asked soberly.

"'Store Man' cannot tell Chief the day to go to battle. 'Store Man' cannot say to Chief of Ibo Tribe, 'You go now to fight Ashanti.' 'Store Man' not Ibo chief. 'Store Man' only trader like Abdee."

"Will you have more people for me before the days of rain?"

"You come back to Africa before days of rain?"

Abdee stood in front of the palm hut now. He ran one hand through his long blond hair paled by the sun and ocean's salt sprays. He answered, "If 'Store Man' gives me his word that he will have more slaves for me—many, many slaves—by the days of long rains I will return for them. But I will only return for many slaves. Not a short string like today."

"I have long string for you. Abdee come. I hear by drums that Abdee's ship sits here in water. I bring many strings of niggers to Abdee to take away in ship. I sell not to English. Not to French. Not to Spanish with gold rings through their ears. I keep slaves for Abdee. I teach my son to sell slaves only to Abdee."

Turning toward the slave coffle, "Store Man" waved his burled staff for one of the guards to join him, a young man whose short but muscular body was covered only by a piece of fabric twisted around his groin. He wore a tricorne hat like "Store Man's" but the hat was garishly decorated with parrot feathers and dried grass. He sauntered toward Abdee and his father, groping with one hand at the fabric twisted around the bulk of his groin.

Putting a hand on the young man's sinewy shoulder, "Store Man" proudly announced, "This is my son. Oldest son I train to sell you slaves. I teach him loyalty. 'Store Man' teaches son good. Son will carry

'Store Man's' ways long after 'Store Man' leaves this earth. Someday 'Store Man's' son trades with Abdee's son. They plant their seed together and make business like 'Store Man' and Abdee do."

Nodding at his father's words, then grinning knowingly at Abdee, the near-naked youth continued to work his hand over the groin cloth and agreed, "Plant seed. Plant seed with white man."

Participating in the act called "planting seed"—a practise of certain Africans from mountain tribes to masturbate at the conclusion of a trade or bargaining—had repelled Abdee in the past when he had done it with "Store Man." Only the prize of valuable slaves made him do it. The prospect of masturbating today with both "Store Man" and his son disgusted Abdee even more so. He fleetingly thought of protesting against the proposal. Remembering his need for "Store Man's" slaves in the future, though, Abdee forced himself to agree to it. He knew that "Store Man" was getting old. This surly young African might soon become the official trader for the Ibo chief.

Studying the youth so eager to participate in the manly act, Abdee soberly asked "Store Man," "Does your son have his father's eye for strong slaves?"

"You see what son has. Son has manhood to match Abdee's," the old man chuckled. He then pushed the youth toward the hut, ordering, "We go see white man's gifts. We all plant seed to make work tree grow big." He then groped his own crotch through the folds of his dingy white robe as he moved across the sand with his son.

Taking a deep breath, Abdee glanced at the tilting flag pole. He saw that the shreds of the Union Jack were flapping more briskly in the breeze. The wind was building. He must not waste precious time.

Turning toward the indigo sea becoming rough

with silver caps, he waved to the *Petit Jour* anchored in the mouth of the cove, signalling his crew to row ashore in shallops and collect these last slaves.

Then, dreading the prospect of stripping himself naked with two other males, Abdee slowly followed "Store Man" and his son toward the hut. He strongly disliked any acts of homosexuality and "Store Man's" son seemed too anxious to partake in what had once been a solemn occasion for the Ibo tribe. Abdee did not like males of any age who stared with such interest at another's manhood.

* * *

The inside of the low-ceilinged hut was thick with green flies. The air smelled both sweet from decaying fruit and rancid from the body odors of black caboceers who had already come here to choose their payment. A shaft of sunlight cut through the narrow door, falling upon the remaining goods heaped in a far corner.

"Store Man" left his son by the door and padded across the dirt floor, carefully appraising the pile of iron kettles, baskets of glass beads, skeins of ribbons, and sabres sheathed in cheap but ornately tooled tin scabbards.

Also ignoring the youth, Abdee moved to another corner of the hut and kicked back a tarpaulin with the toe of his black boot. He bent to lift a hemp bag from the floor and, reaching inside the bag, he pulled out lengths of violet, blue, red, and green silk.

Throwing the fabric onto the dirt floor like haphazard bands of a rainbow, Abdee called to "Store Man," "This silk is worth more than the few prisoners you brought me today. But I keep my promise to a friend. You must keep your promise to me next time. You must also teach your son to honor promises."

Seeing the silk, "Store Man" dropped the burled staff to the floor and fell to his knees. He ran his bony hands over the crumpled fabric, murmuring with saliva beading in the corners of his blue-black lips, "Silk . . . thin like water . . ."

"Silk," the youth repeated from the door. He had freed his manhood from the cloth and squeezed his greasy black hardness with the pink undersides of his fingers. "Silk good for woman. Silk make woman happy. *Man* make woman happy!" He bounded the hardness of his thick penis in the flat of his hand, grinning widely and showing even lines of stark white teeth.

Continuing to ignore the youth, Abdee listened now to the sound of raucous shouts and the clanking of chains outside the hut. His crew had arrived to begin taking the Africans to their shelves in the ship's hold.

Not wanting to waste too much time here indulging "Store Man's" custom, Abdee finally reached for the crotch of his doeskin breeches. He began to work his hand over the bulge of his own midsection. He quickly looked again toward the African youth, seeing him smoothing back the skin of his phallus and cupping his other hand under the pendulous bag of his scrotum.

Still trying to ignore the boy's prurient attitude to this meeting, Abdee turned to "Store Man" and called in a sober voice, "You promise to bring me no less than three hundred slaves next time, 'Store Man'?"

Kneeling in front of the silks, "Store Man" nodded his head, agreeing, "Three hundred niggers. But there will be little niggers in three hundred."

Abdee liked the idea of buying healthy children. He said, "Children grow into strong workers. White masters feed them well. But no small babies, 'Store

Man.' They need their mothers. Bring me children who can walk. No sick. No wounded. No babies who need their mothers."

"Store Man" now gave Abdee one of his own conditions for the next barter. He said, "You bring long guns when you return. Long guns that spill blood and bags of thunder to feed long guns."

Abdee moved to lower his breeches as he agreed. "Tell your chief that I will pay him one long gun for every ten good niggers he sends me. One for ten. He will thank you for making him the richest, most powerful chief of all the mountain tribes."

The young man had moved closer at the sight of Abdee's naked groin. He pushed his midsection forward as if he wanted to compare sizes of masculinity, to see the largeness of his black penis compared to Abdee's lighter-skinned organ.

Abdee moved one step back. He did not want to speak harshly to the boy, to tell him to keep a distance and risk upsetting his proud father.

Rising slowly to his feet, "Store Man" clutched for the soiled hem of his robe with one hand and tucked the folds into a leather belt around his waist. He nodded with approval at his son's fine show of potency.

The boy dropped both arms to his side, his taut penis bobbing freely in front of him. He reached with one hand to grip Abdee's penis, to assist him in the act.

Abdee stood farther back. He tried to control his temper.

Gripping his own penis, "Store Man" began to squeeze it in his bony fist, saying " 'Store Man' . . . Abdee . . . old friends, mix their seed again. 'Store Man' brings Abdee three hundred good niggers. Abdee takes these today. Abdee brings gun and food to make thunder. Abdee . . . 'Store Man' . . . 'Store

Man's' son all mix seed today to make work-tree big."

Abdee closed his eyes and repeated "Store Man's" words as if accepting a formal toast. "We all plant our seed today to make work-tree big." Rather than this mountain ritual, though, he was thinking about a woman, straining for an image to make his masculinity erect. He was trying to forget that he was here in this hut masturbating with two men, an old man and his anxious son.

Slowly, the vision of the tall Ashanti woman began to fill Abdee's mind. He was visualizing the young widow whom "Store Man" had called "Kinga." He was remembering the patch of black wool fixed between her slim legs.

Remembering how her vagina had clamped his middle finger, Abdee imagined her contracting muscles satisfying his masculinity. He foresaw how he would train her to be his love slave. He envisioned the tips of her brown fingers holding back the lips of her vagina. There was a pinkness beneath the black wiry hair. He could almost feel her wetness.

His phallus began to build. The blood rushed toward the crown, forming a hard knob on the end of his thickness as he imagined himself inching into Kinga . . .

Beside him, "Store Man" praised, "Look! Abdee built big like nigger boy. Abdee built big like son."

The young man agreed in a throaty voice. His cupped fist slicked back and forth on his own masculinity. Watching Abdee swell into a hard and thick pole of taut skin, seeing his thick fingers move over the still growing organ in assured strokes, the youth began to take deeper breaths. He jutted his midsection forward; the muscles tensed across the flatness of his ebony stomach; he was building as large as Abdee and, wanting to share this sight which was so erotic to him, he shouted, "Look, Abdee, Look!"

The words were not spoken quickly enough. Abdee still kept his eyes clenched shut, his mind fixed on Kinga. And it was then—at the sound of the young African's voice—that soft, pearly drops of sperm spurted in crisscrossing arcs onto the dirt floor of the hut. "Store Man" himself joined the explosion, stimulated by the potency of his eldest son. The pact was completed, finalizing the sale of fifty Ashanti slaves to Richard Abdee, marking enslavement for three hundred more Negroes to be seized from their mountain villages within the next three months, and insuring a future of trading between Abdee and a new generation of African slave dealers.

* * *

Kinga. The name which the birdlike Ibo trader had called her on the beach meant nothing to Sabata Abadie. She had first seen the black man in the three-cornered hat when she had been kneeling over the dead body of her husband in the forest after the Ibo warriors had attacked the village during the stillness of *betwabere*—the time for cutting palm trees.

That day now seemed an eternity away. But Sabata Abadie had not had an opportunity in that time to cover herself with funeral dust nor to prepare her husband's *boaboa* to send away his spirit. The black caboceer and his cruel Ibo guards had locked wooden rings around the wrists of the Ashantis who had not been killed, chaining them together as prisoners. The dirt now caking Sabata Abadie's face and body had come from the voyage from the mountains to this endless river which showed no bank on the other side.

Sabata Abadie had heard about this big river from her husband. He had also told her strange men with white faces were taking many Africans away from *Abidiri*, the homeland of all black people.

The Ashantis also captured slaves from other tribes but they kept their slaves in their villages. They treated them as people. Slavery had been a fact of life in *Abidiri* for hundreds of years—but never to be bartered into slavery like cattle and taken away from this homeland.

Life had suddenly become a death world to Sabata Abadie. She had been brought to a nether world where ragged palm huts lined the sandy bank of an endless river. Where white men prodded their fingers into her womanhood. Where wide canoes carried them across the water to a floating prison. There was a deep pit within this floating prison where Sabata Abadie now lay on her back, locked by iron chains into a space no bigger than the hollow trunk of a fallen tree.

Despite the darkness of this floating prison, Sabata Abadie knew that Ashantis were not the only people chained down here in the humid black space. She had seen rows of other captives, men and women lined on shelves, their feet or hands protruding from the blackness. She had heard them whispering, knowing they came from many tribes.

You are Ashanti, she told herself in the cramped darkness of this floating prison. *Your husband is dead. He left you no children and you must be thankful for that now. You must act strong in the future for your husband's spirit. Your strength will be his boaboa. It is now your duty to help his people. Pra was his only enemy in the tribe. Pra might not help you. You have to win Pra for a friend or fight him like you will fight the white men. You must be both a woman and a warrior. To this new life of death, you must say "Aba-oo." Welcome.*

2

THE "PETIT JOUR"

Rugged, weatherbeaten, its black paint dulled by sea spray, the *Petit Jour* was a three-masted galley fitted with swivel cannons to fire toward quartering ships or against slaves on deck. She had been built in Liverpool to carry supplies from England to the Virginias. Abdee had bought the vessel from a failing trading company on the island of Nevis. He replaced the riggings, caulked the hull, renamed her the *Petit Jour*, and the trader quickly transformed into both a supply ship to carry food, water, hardware to *Castelo Novo Mundo* and a slaver for his trans-Atlantic voyages.

The captain was Thomas Pennington, a fat-bellied Englishman with ginger hair and muttonchop whiskers. Abdee had hired Pennington two years ago on the island of Barbados after a personal scandal involving a Negro youth had cost the English captain his job aboard a brigantine out of Bridgetown.

Richard Abdee and Thomas Pennington had little

in common except for the safe Atlantic passages of the *Petit Jour*. They normally spoke but once a day throughout a voyage, meeting on the quarterdeck while the prisoners were brought from the ship's hold for their food, airing, and exercises.

Thomas Pennington never outwardly admitted to Abdee that he did not approve of slave-trading. He himself only owned a personal slave, a cabin boy he called "Robby."

Abdee suspected that Captain Pennington still practised what seamen call the "Greek Vice," the weakness for young boys which had cost him his job out of Barbados. The fact that Robby did very little work for Pennington corroborated Abdee's suspicions that the Negro youth slept in the Captain's cabin for reasons other than to perform the normal services of a lackey to the corpulent, gingerhaired Englishman.

* * *

The first week of the westward voyage passed without incident. The *Petit Jour* had ridden a strong wind from the African coast, now travelling full-sailed on an Atlantic sea-lane toward a horizon banked with billowy white clouds.

A few sailors stood on deck today, around the mizzenmast holding long guns. Only one of the swivel cannon was manned to fire against the Negroes in case of trouble, a precaution not yet needed since leaving Port Weston.

Always cautious, Abdee felt uneasy about the perfect weather. Distrusting people as much as Nature, he also worried about the Africans obeying every command on deck. This immediate subservience troubled him.

It was normal for many prisoners to refuse their food at the outset of a voyage, preferring to starve themselves to death rather than to be taken as slaves. This problem was so commonplace on an African voyage, that Abdee kept metal clamps aboard the *Petit Jour*, mouth screws which could be fitted against a slave's gums to open their mouths for nourishment to be stuffed down their throats.

Also, Africans often tried to escape during the first days of their exercise schedule on deck, giving a wild shriek and jumping overboard in hopes of swimming back to Africa. Abdee kept himself prepared for this behavior, too. He willingly sacrificed the lives of a few people at the beginning of the voyage, letting the other blacks see with their own eyes that there was no place to swim to, that their chains would weight them down into the lapping ocean.

By the beginning of this second week out of Africa, though, not one man nor woman had made a break for the railing. Abdee mentioned the fact today to Captain Pennington as they stood together on the quarterdeck. They were watching the black people jump up and down, swinging their arms like windmills, then moving toward the wooden food tubs placed along the starboard where they would eat a mixture of rice and cured pork called "dab-a-dab."

Pennington stood with his hands folded behind the back of his blue frock coat, gazing down at the collection of half-naked bucks and wenches. He answered in a lofty tone, "I think we have the Lord to thank for their blessed obedience, Mister Abdee."

Pennington's religious attitudes sickened Abdee. He did not mind Pennington clinging to his Bible, quoting Scripture like a spinster to his cabin boy, but he did wish that Pennington would not bring his personal beliefs to the deck.

Abdee said, "I'm mentioning this strange conduct to you because I thought it might mean trouble." The

Africans finished their exercises as Abdee spoke to Pennington, then moved toward their wooden food tubs. One woman among the prisoners attracted Abdee's eyes. He watched her squat in front of a wooden tub, slowly cupping handfuls of dab-a-dab into her mouth. She stopped to suck on one of the limes provided for the slaves at meal time, the citric acid being a safeguard against scurvy as well as quenching thirsts. Abdee had been studying the same woman every day since leaving Africa. She was the Ashanti woman whom he called Kinga.

"Trouble?" Pennington said. He shook his head. "If I understand your meaning, Mister Abdee, you are crediting your cargo with a common language. There are many tribes down there. They cannot communicate as easily as you might believe."

"There's more that binds people together than language," Abdee grumbled, wishing that Pennington would be less argumentative like an old woman, more assertive like a man.

"Mister Abdee," Pennington began slowly, holding his nose high to catch the sea air, "if you are thinking that there is some tribal witchcraft afoot in the humid confines of this hold, some *juju* or religious spells being worked from a common African god, no . . ." He shook his head.

"I am not talking about witchcraft, voodoo, or *juju* curses. Blacks are religious people but these are prisoners. They're being taken away from a home they'll never see again. They're going to be slaves for the rest of their lives. I always think about what *I* would do if *I* were in their place. What would *I* be plotting if some strangers were carrying me across the sea in chains?"

Abdee kept his eyes on Kinga as he spoke, seeing that the recent days at sea had not taken a toll on her attractiveness. Her skin still retained its ebony gloss. Her face remained proud and impassive. The sun caught the sheen of her hair plaited like twists of black silk against her skull. She knelt, almost elegantly, at the mush barrel as if it were a tribal banquet.

Pennington said, "I cannot speak for what a man like yourself would do in such circumstances, Mister Abdee. I can only hazard a guess that your captives might very well be praying for the deliverance of their . . . souls."

"I thought good Christians like yourself, Captain Pennington, believed that Africans do not have souls."

Pausing before he answered, Pennington cocked his head and finally admitted, "I personally believe that Africans are heathen. But I believe they can be saved. Greater miracles have been wrought."

"Captain Pennington, perhaps you and I have at long last found something we have in common. You believe that Africans can be taught the Christian religion. So you must believe they are human. I believe niggers are human, too. But in a slightly different way than you. I believe a nigger will stab you in the back as soon as you turn away from him. That they are dangerous. Deadly. And stubborn. In fact, Captain Pennington, I believe niggers are like most white men I know."

Still holding his eyes on the starboard, Abdee watched the crew lead the first group of prisoners back toward the hatch. He noticed Kinga's effortless movement as she descended the ladder. He saw how her breasts stood firmly inside her soiled body cloth. The proud way she held her head. That the iron mannacles seemed unimportant to her.

Forgetting momentarily about the personal rule he had set for himself of never mating with a black woman on a slave crossing, Abdee's masculinity began to stir inside his breeches. He wondered if he should break his rule. Should he have Kinga brought to his cabin? Was that wise? Or would it be foolish, too risky to take this woman so early in her captivity? If she screamed, attacked him, made any show of disobedience against him, Abdee knew that he would have to kill her. He could do no less and retain authority.

Yes, he decided that it would be wiser to wait until he reached the castle and trained Kinga properly in the secrecy of the Barracoon. She was the kind of strong-willed woman who fascinated him. She would be a challenge to dominate.

Disrupting Abdee's thoughts at that moment, Pennington asked with a forced casualness, "This seems an opportune time to mention a matter which I have been intending to speak to you about, Mister Abdee. In our original agreement, you told me that I could have occasional use of your ship and crew while you were not using her. When you reach the castle, will you keep your vessel there or can I take her to Dominica? It would be for no more than two days at the most. I have some personal . . . business I must attend to in Portsmouth."

"I can't make any promises now, Pennington. However, I will be needing supplies for the castle. You could collect and deliver them for me. Now, if you will excuse me, I must return to my cabin and finish logging the last slaves we bought at Port Weston. Tonight the crew begins choosing women from the captvies. The sailors sometimes get rough. I want an accurate record of every slave in case a woman gets hurt. A valuable wench sometimes becomes maimed—even killed—and I want to list their prices in case I have to deduct the cost from a crewman's pay."

Turning from Pennington, Abdee walked toward his cabin, making a mental note to tell his first mate, Samuel Tewes, to threaten any man with a severe flogging if they so much as touched the Ashanti woman. Kinga was to be saved for him and him alone.

Also, Abdee made a mental note to find out from Thomas Pennington about the nature of the business he had to conduct in Portsmouth. He did not like anyone—in his employ or bondage—doing anything without his knowledge.

*   *   *

In the past eight days, Sabata Abadie had tried to persuade Pra to help her to speak to the people from the other tribes. Pra could speak other tongues than Ashanti. Sabata Abadie begged him to forget their old differences and help her teach everyone down here in the hold that they were one people bonded by the color of their skin. The children of *Abidiri* must unite as one tribe.

Sabata Abadie had been able to answer few specific questions which the people asked her in the last days. She did not know how long they would be held prisoners in the belly of this ship. She could not say where their destination would be. She only repeated stories which her husband had told her about the vastness of the ocean. She begged men not to throw themselves into the water when they were taken up on deck for exercise. Not even the strongest swimmer could swim back to their homeland. She was pleased so far that some of her words were taken seriously.

Pra had his own ideas for survival aboard this slave ship. He whispered to the people, telling them that they should keep their eyes alert for ways to steal weapons from the white men. He preached that everyone should look for sharp instruments to break the iron chains which held them to the wooden shelves. He reminded the black people that they outnumbered the whites, that they could seize control of the ship and force it to take them back to *Abidiri*.

Sabata Abadie violently disagreed with Pra's beliefs. She waited until late at night, long after she heard the last footsteps on deck, to begin her arguments with Pra. Sabata Abadie believed that the black people's strength now must be spent on keeping one another in good health and spirits. They had no medicine, no healing herbs or feather charms. When they were taken up to deck for their exercises and food, she urged the healthy ones to stand aside so that the white men could see the sickly prisoners. She explained that the white men did not want them to die. They wanted the black people to be like healthy cattle because that was how they would be sold or traded—like cattle—when they reached their destination. She said that unlike the slaves which Africans took in battle and kept in their villages, the white men sold their slaves to other white men.

But then came tonight's mystery. Not Sabata Abadie nor any of the black people, could understand at first why the white men came down to the hold with iron keys tonight, unlocking some of them from their chains and taking them away from the wooden shelves. When she realized that only females were being chosen by the white men, the reason suddenly became apparent. Unlike black people, the white men had no scruples about imposing themselves on a woman taken in a slave raid.

Sabata Abadie saw girls too young to have full breasts and middle-aged woman who were almost grandmothers pulled from the shelves. She heard the agony of fathers, husbands, and brothers as they lay locked in chains watching their wives and sisters being mauled in front of them.

Waiting for the men to unlock her from the chains, too, Sabata Abadie prepared herself for rape. But the white men only stared at her body, smirking at her as they stroked her long legs with hands as rough as a lizard's scales. But they did not include her with the other females.

Finally, Sabata Abadie understood why they left her locked in the ship's heaving darkness. One man leered at her and said in a rasping voice two names which she understood. "Kinga . . . Abdee's wench!"

Kinga. The name referred to her. The Ibo caboceer had called her "Kinga" on the bank of the endless river.

Sabata Abadie also remembered the other name—Abdee. The Ibo caboceer had called the white man with yellow hair by that name, the white man who had prodded his coarse finger between her legs.

When Sabata Abadie pictured Abdee in her mind, she saw a white man she wanted to kill with a bush knife. She remembered seeing selfishness in his face. His eyes were like blue pools poisoned with evilness.

Pressing the repellent thought from her mind that Abdee was saving her for himself, Sabata Abadie worked to console the husbands, brothers, and fathers who had watched their women being dragged away from them. The screams above them did not make her task simple but she persisted in trying to make them understand that they all were now property of the white men, warning them that they must expect worse degradations.

When the sailors shoved the women down the ladder tonight and relocked them in their shelves, Sabata Abadie met her most difficult task. Some women were too hysterical to speak. Others sobbed about the abuse they had suffered from the white men. Those men near the women listened to the stories, cursing the wicked whites. Other men passed the stories down to the next person lying on a shelf.

A Kru maiden with eyes as white as new ivory beads gasped how two men had held her by the arms while a third man spread open her legs, ramming himself into her vagina with no care for injuries or even enjoyment. She said he had had the feelings of a *bagya*, a jungle animal . . .

One Mundingo woman had been bound to a pole with ropes, her legs secured wide apart by manacles while a succession of men took turns satisfying themselves with her. She cursed them all with an evil *greegree*.

A pubescent girl had been smeared with grease to take the sexual enormity of a sailor covered with hair like a flying monkey.

More than one woman whispered stories how the sailors had preferred to mate them from behind, ripping into their anus in an unnatural act.

Sabata Abadie suffered through each and every pitiful report, waiting until the hysterics ebbed before she began her most difficult task. She talked openly about the shame of carrying a white man's child. She assured the women who had been raped that she would prepare a nostrum to abort a white man's child.

Next, she tried to convince the females who had suffered unnatural acts that they had been the victims of better fortune. Their body wounds would heal. She urged all the women to find a way to satisfy the white men which would not plant a child in their wombs.

Pra cursed her violently for spreading this advice, saying that she urged depravities among good women, influencing young girls to encourage evil, chastizing her for not respecting the sancity of the family.

Sabata Abadie laughed bitterly at Pra's opinions. She answered that it was better for a black woman to take a white man in her mouth—or squirm her buttocks to satisfy his lusts—rather than to carry an unwanted infant in her body for nine months, to bear a child whose head she might be tempted to beat upon the rocks.

Life had changed, Sabata Abadie argued. It was useless to wish for families now. Or did Pra think that the white men were going to sell families and lovers together? That an African family would be allowed to continue in the world where they were being taken like animals?

Then, to add conviction to her words, Sabata Abadie coldly stated that she had decided to renounce her African name. No longer would she be called Sabata Abadie. All white people were her enemy and she wanted them to know exactly who would seek revenge on them. Let them call her "Kinga." Let them know exactly who drained the blood from their veins and drank it from a calabash bowl. *Kinga.*

❊   ❊   ❊

Captain Pennington lay awake in his cabin that night long after the cries from the African women died down on deck; an hour had passed since the last sailor had stumbled in a drunken stupor to the berths.

Dressed in a voluminous white cotton night shirt, Pennington cradled Robby's naked chest in the crook of his arm. The silver moonlight streamed through a mullioned window as Pennington spoke to his sleeping cabin boy in hushed tones, occasionally leaning forward to brush his wooly head with dry kisses.

"The Lord has given you to me, my midnight cherub, and I finally recognize my duty to take you away from this foul atmosphere. Richard Abdee is Satan. His crew, a band of licentious demons.

"The Lord more than approves the love between us, beloved boy. He foresaw it. A cleric in Portsmouth has agreed to join us in a religious ceremony. I failed in similar plans once because the Lord had not deemed it right for me. The Almighty shamed me publicly to test my fortitude. I see now that the Lord predestined you as my only happiness . . .

"Ebony cherub, I shall soon give you not only your freedom when we take our nuptials, but my name as well. I will share my life with you as readily as you share your youth with me . . ."

Leaning to kiss the boy again on the head, Pennington whispered, "Rest now, beloved. Leave the details of our future to the Lord, myself, and the holy man in Portsmouth. The Lord has plans for our future . . . and may the Almighty also show me a way to deliver Abdee to his hellfire."

Before he leaned his head back on the pillow to fall asleep, though, Pennington could not resist reaching between Robby's legs to cup the warmth of his penis and scrotum in his hand. He craved Robby to mount him as if the black boy were the man and Pennington his passive partner. It was with those thoughts that Pennington finally put his hatred for Abdee from his mind and drifted off into a blissful sleep.

3

THE FLOGGING

The *Petit Jour* began trimming her sails off the island of Tobago. The winds carried a sweet tropical smell, lighter than the raw and salty gusts from the open sea; the water transformed from silver-capped blackness into a turquoise mirror; more islands soon appeared in the distance—Grenada, Barbados, Mustique, many smaller islands still not charted or named on any map, only verdant smells on the horizon telling that the Atlantic Ocean had finally led into the Caribbean, that the sea-lanes were finally approaching the first land in the West Indies, the Windward Islands.

The closer that Abdee got to home, the more he thought about the life awaiting him at *Castelo Novo Mundo*. Two months were too long to be at sea, sleeping aboard a tossing ship, swatting pestilent mosquitoes, eating food little better than the dab-a-dab mush given to the prisoners. He would soon be waking up to the crowing of a rooster, smelling the tempting aroma of freshly baked bread drifting from the castle's kitchen, basking in the morning sun on one of the many terraces, discussing the day's plans with his overseer, Magnus.

Richard Abdee realized that the life he had built for himself in the last eight years at *Castelo Novo Mundo* would seem monastic, even grim to many men. The Portuguese fortress isolated him from the outside world but afforded little space to roam. Its vastness ran perpendicular rather than the rolling, wide horizons he had known on Dragonard Plantation on the island of St. Kitts.

A man could not ride a horse at *Castelo Novo Mundo*. There were no fields, gardens or orchards to explore. The earth had been transported as ballast in ships, dumped on the terraces and cultivated by Abdee's slaves to provide a modicum of fresh vegetables.

Abdee still kept a curtain over those years in which he had counted his fertile soil by miles instead of yards, the days when he had been the master of more than five hundred slaves on a sugar plantation. He had gained control of a plantation in one short year but lost it in a single night. He still had nightmares about that slave uprising. He still saw the burning ceiling fall from the center garden, engulfing his Negress lover in flames. He wondered if Kinga could ever match Naomi in spirit? In excitement? In exchanges of masterly lusts? Naomi had been the only woman whom Abdee had truly enjoyed. He still saw her in desperate nightmares, hearing her laughter pierce the night, then turn to screams of agony as the burning ceiling fell . . .

But, Abdee was not a man who admitted defeat. Nor did he ever reevaluate the one goal which had raged inside him as a young man when he first came to the West Indies from England—to control his own destiny. He remained content as long as no person in his command disobeyed an order, when there was always a plentiful stock of women to satisfy his lustful cravings.

During the last two months away from home, Abdee had ached for sexual satisfaction. Because he disliked the smell of cattle manure which clung to most coastal African women, though, and knowing that the Negresses at Port Weston were riddled with venereal disease, Abdee never lay with a woman in Africa.

Abdee also remained true to his resolution of not rutting with a Negress aboard the *Petit Jour*. The only female who tempted him on this trip was Kinga but, recognizing her rebellious spirit, he did not want to chance her disobedience. He would wait until they reached the castle to begin training her and, only then, could she ever replace Naomi.

Great personal discipline was required to remain celibate on a slave voyage. Abdee tried not to listen to the ribald laughter, the lustful groans, the cries which covered the deck from stern to prow at night when the sailors satisfied themselves in drunken revelries.

Yet, always the next morning, some man inevitably recounted a teasing story about an encounter he had enjoyed, a scuffle with one of the frightened Negresses, the submissions which the sailor eventually enjoyed.

During the last few mornings of this voyage, though, Abdee had heard strange tales about the Negresses in this particular cargo. The black wenches had begun to show a preference for using their mouths on the men rather than to let them ride between their legs. The men who enjoyed sodomy with a female bragged to Abdee that these African women had stopped fighting their perverse advances.

Hearing these stories, Abdee remembered how

this cargo of slaves also ate their food so obediently. That they had never tried to throw themselves overboard throughout the entire trip. And, now, many women were practising perverse sexual actions which they would normally abhor.

Wondering more than ever about what kind of strange prisoners he was bringing back from Africa, Abdee decided to observe them more closely. He would go down into the hold.

* * *

Richard Abdee stood in the dark shadows at the base of the ladder, resting one hand on the pistol tucked into his belt and tried not to breathe the air reaking with vomit, urine, and excrement. He stared down the double line of shelves which held the slaves in a "spoon" fashion, a manner which the head of one prisoner alternated with the feet of another.

Abdee never tried to flatter himself that he ran a model slave ship. A slaver was only praiseworthy when Negroes were crowded into the hull, promising the owner a vast fortune on the sales block. In that aspect, this voyage was a disappointment. Abdee wanted all the money he could get to buy land on one of the larger islands, to rebuild the empire he had lost with the destruction of Dragonard Plantation.

Forgetting about the strange behavior of this cargo, he stood at the base of the ladder and began to calculate the sum he thought the four hundred and fifty slaves would fetch in a market. He needed at least one hundred dollars per head to feel satisfied, anything less would be consumed by the costs of food, wages for the crew, scores of other niggling expenses.

His calculations were suddenly disturbed by an argument, the exchange of angry whispers ahead of him in the darkness of the slave shelves. He strained his ears to hear, quickly recognizing the conversation as a disagreement among the slaves.

The idea that miserable prisoners still had the stamina to argue and fight among themselves amused Abdee. It confirmed his beliefs about despicability of all human nature.

Soon, he discerned one shrill voice rising above the others. He next heard the quick rattle of irons and, in the daylight spilling through the deck, he saw a pair of manacles raise from a middle shelf to strike the head of another slave.

Quickly drawing his pistol, Abdee strode down the slippery boards. He shouted for the argument to stop. Damn! He did not need these niggers killing one another, detracting from his small profit . . . He glanced at the surprised face of the Negro who held his black hands ready to strike.

He stopped, staring at the gashed cheeks of the black attacker. It was Pra; the Ashanti craftsman who "Store Man" had given him as a gift. Pra was going to strike a woman with his manacled hands. He was fighting with . . . Kinga!

Coshing Pra's head with his pistol butt, Abdee cursed the African. He jerked away Pra's manacled hands when he tried to protect himself. The clomp of boots immediately sounded overhead. Abdee was soon surrounded by members of his crew, Samuel Tewes anxiously waiting for an order to discipline the Negro.

Nodding at Pra, Abdee ordered, "Bring this black son-of-a-bitch up on deck. Lash him to the mast. Have my whip ready."

Before leaving, Abdee turned to Kinga. He saw her staring at him with alarm. Although her usual coolness was temporarily shattered, she did not look at Abdee with grateful eyes. What kind of female was she?

Abruptly turning, Abdee moved down the shelves and climbed the ladder toward the deck. He tried to contain his fury, telling himself that he must not kill Pra, that he must control the anger which often overtook him like a madman's seizure.

Planting his feet firmly on the gently tossing deck, he grasped the oily whip in his hand. He glared at Pra secured to the mizzenmast and sneered, "You bastard, if you would have as much as scratched that woman . . ."

The first lash cracked against Pra's back, two neat trails of blood quickly forming on his dull black skin. Abdee was using the whip with a splayed tip, the Dragonard's whip which had been the tool of the public whipmaster in the main square in Basseterre, St. Kitts.

Striking a second, third, and fourth time in quick succession, Abdee lost all control over regulating his strokes. He could no longer contain his hatred. He had not wanted Pra in the first place. He thought about Kinga, how this despicable slave could have prevented him from enjoying the only woman he was saving for himself. He imagined Pra striking Kinga's skull with iron, spilling her brains onto the boards.

Abdee's fury soon intermingled with sensual thoughts of Kinga; his mind flashed with punishment for Pra and erotic images of Kinga, how he would break her like a young colt, watching her slowly learning to acknowledge him as her master.

As the sound of the splayed whip continued to land against Pra's naked back, Abdee's needs for revenge against Pra increased his lust for Kinga. His penis began to expand inside his breeches. His heart beat faster. His eyes dulled to a blue, lifeless grey.

Finally, hearing the count of twenty-nine, Abdee lowered the whip and stood staring at the bloody flesh hanging from Pra's mutilated back. It was then that he realized that Pra had not once screamed for mercy.

Abdee raised the whip with a loud crack. Pra flinched. Abdee knew from this that Pra had not lost consciousness. That he was a stubborn man, a true Ashanti, a man unwilling to beg for mercy.

"Untie him," Abdee gasped, turning away from the mast. "Wash him. Rub some oil in the wounds. Take him back to the hold. And tie him on his stomach. Let them all see the whip marks."

Recoiling the Dragonard whip, Abdee glanced down at his doeskin breeches and saw the potent bulge of his masculinity. He was as hard as iron. That had not changed from his younger days. He was pleased with that.

*   *   *

As the late afternoon sun hovered orange to the larboard of the *Petit Jour,* Abdee saw a small speck ahead of him in the sea, a mound which took on monolithic proportions as the ship drew nearer, a bulk incongruous to the gentle line of the pastel horizon. The distant object looked too solid to be another ship; its position on the seascape was bulky, immobile, yet strangely permanent. It was *Castelo Novo Mundo.*.

Staring soberly at the dark shape jutting from the sea, Abdee soon discerned its castellated towers, the deep gashes in the stone which served as windows, the rocks which surrounded the base like enormous chunks of jagged black glass.

The wooden portcullis to the castle's harbor was

already raised when the *Petit Jour* moved toward the entrance. The ship's rigging creaked; the ropes sang on their spools; the spars strained against the wind as the prow now inched toward a long shadow cast by the stone tower across the turquoise water.

It was not until the ship had moved completely into the afternoon darkness cast by *Castelo Novo Mundo* that Abdee saw three vessels anchored inside the harbor.

Cautious about the privateers who still roamed the Caribbean, he immediately looked toward their masts to see their flags. Pirates usually flew the colors of Tortuga. He saw instead the guidons of Spain, France and America.

Next, spotting a figure excitedly jumping up and down on the slope of the dirt yard, Abdee realized the ships were friendly. Magnus had come to the harbor to welcome the *Petit Jour*.

Relaxing now that he knew for certain that the ships were friendly, Abdee knew almost for certain who they were. No one was allowed inside the castle's walled harbor without a direct—or indirect—invitation.

Before Magnus had time to shout to Abdee on the forecastle, the dirt yard became alive with black people. Abdee's people swarmed from the many wooden doors, and gates, and posterns opening onto the yard. Old ladies with bright cotton turbans waddled up from the cellars. Half-naked bucks rushed from the tool shops. Ripe wenches appeared with bundles on their heads, flashing welcoming smiles. Small children waved their arms.

Standing with one hand tucked into the waist band of his doeskin breeches, Abdee returned his people's greeting with a half-wave. Then, stepping back from the bow, he disappeared among the confusion spreading on the deck. He did not yet want to meet his guests. And when he did choose the right time to greet them, he would pretend as if their presence here was a complete surprise to him. Act as if he had not arranged for Hugh Tyler, Ignatio Soto, and Claude Saint-Barbot to come to *Castelo Novo Mundo*.

4

THE BARRACOON

The lowest depths of *Castelo Novo Mundo* were honeycombed with rooms, stairways, and passages, some rooms being great halls with vaulted ceilings and expansive mosaic pavings, but the majority were nothing more than lewens with straw-covered floors, cubicles barely tall enough for a person to stand.

After being chained again into coffles, the African slaves were led up the ladder from the hold, across the larboard, down the narrow gangplank, and herded through the crowd of goggle-eyed castle slaves collected in the dirt yard.

Dragging their chains down a winding stone stairway, the slaves emerged in the dark area of the castle which lay far below the water line of the Caribbean. Pitch torches flickered on the walls of hewn stone. The air smelled of age-old must. Daylight never pentetrated these subterranean dungeons known as The Barracoon.

Pra was the last slave to be taken from the shelves in the hold. Abdee saw that he was confined to an isolated cell in The Barracoon and that the old crone, Lolly Mumba, was put in charge of administering healing ointments to his back wounds. Lolly Mumba acted as midwife, nurse, surgeon, occasionally even voodoo priestess at *Castelo Novo Mundo*. Abdee considered that she might even suggest what to do with Pra, whether he should die or live. That decision, though, could wait for the moment.

Abdee spoke only momentarily with Captain Pennington as the slaves were being unloaded from the ship, telling him to consult the Afro-Spanish cook, Consuela, about any provisions she needed from Portsmouth. He told Pennington to leave at dawn the next morning and, as the island Dominica was only a short distance to the north, he demanded that the *Petit Jour* be back at the castle no later than forty-eight hours from that evening.

When he bluntly asked Pennington what business he had to do in Portsmouth, and Pennington said that it involved visiting a clergyman from Wales who had a small mission there, Abdee dismissed any further interrogations. He did not want to hear more religious talk. He was not interested in clerics. How could they affect his future, the pending sale of African slaves, his dream for re-establishing himself on earth more fertile than the rocks here at *Castelo Novo Mundo*?

❖   ❖   ❖

Abdee planned to work throughout the night in the Barracoon, keeping himself awake with strong Peruvian coffee laced with rum, settling the Africans into the subterranean cells which would be home to them until they were sold to one of the three visiting dealers. Having decided by now to withhold twenty-five blacks from the sale, he ordered them to be penned separately from the others. These twenty-five included Pra and Kinga.

The gang bosses at *Castelo Novo Mundo* were mostly small-boned but wiry Negroes from the Ibo Tribe, men adept at controlling prisoners. The four hundred and twenty-five slaves to be sold were soon divided into groups by age and sex. Next, the frightened Africans were bathed in huge wooden vats and examined for diseases and physical imperfections which had gone unnoticed on their purchase. Finally, they were fed a nourishing meal of beef and root vegetables before being shoved into cells where they would sleep in small groups until tomorrow's more rigorous inspections.

Magnus followed Abdee from chamber to chamber, marking entries in a leatherbound journal about each new slave, jotting notes about their ages, signs of stubbornness, physical fitness, conditions of feet and teeth, scribbling notes about any traces of body sores, hearing defects, hemorrhoids.

In between cataloguing the new slaves in the journal, Magnus spoke to Abdee about the three merchants who had arrived here in his absence, reporting that they were gathering in the dining-hall to meet Abdee at the evening meal. That the wife of the American dealer, Anna Tyler, was particularly interested in meeting him.

Abdee had not planned on a woman coming here with her husband. The intrusion angered him. He also scoffed at the idea of having dinner so soon with strangers. He preferred to hear about the visitors first from Magnus. He had already made other plans in his mind for tonight.

The details which Magnus reported about each visitor corroborated the few facts which Abdee already knew. Ignatio Soto was one of the most prosperous slave dealers in Cuba, owning a *mercado* on Havana's *Calle de Esclavos*—the Street of Slaves. Abdee realized that if Soto had come all the way to *Castelo Novo Mundo* and not sent an agent to act on his behalf, he must be willing to pay very high prices. He also knew that Soto was primarily interested in *especialades*, slaves with highly developed skills or extraordinary physical beauty, the category of slaves which sold in English and American markets as "fancies."

Tyler was another important name in the slave world. It was often the practise of the Tyler Auction House on Duvall Street in New Orleans to purchase blacks who were difficult and troublesome. Hugh Tyler resold them for high prices as laborers for rice, cotton, or tobacco plantations where a slave's life expectancy was unnaturally short, seldom lasting past three years.

The man about whom Abdee knew the least was Claude Saint-Barbot from Martinique. He had heard that the Frenchman had only recently become a slave dealer, a man who did not know blacks, a virtual apprentice in the business who could easily be duped. But Abdee was more interested in Saint-Barbot's plantation on Martinique, *Côte Rouge*, than he was in him as a prospective buyer. Abdee had long suspected that *Côte Rouge* might be the very plantation which he hoped to own.

Magnus could provide few further details about Saint-Barbot, except that, unlike the Cuban and American, Saint-Barbot had not spent his time here pursuing black wenches. Magnus added that Saint-Barbot had not tried to seduce any of the young bucks, that he showed no interest in any male or female. That he, apparently, lived a life of celibacy.

Abdee and Magnus now stood in the area of the

Barracoon which the Portuguese had called the *sala de tormenta*, the torture chamber. Abdee would use it tomorrow to oil the new slaves after they received their second bath, restoring a sheen to their now dull black skins with generous applications of palm oil.

Magnus was explaining, "The American, he has the most wenches. He grabs for titty or pussy wherever he sees it passing."

"What about his wife?"

Pausing, Magnus bit his lower lip. He did not immediately answer.

"What's she like?"

Grinning like a little boy, Magnus answered, "Not hot like fire, Master, Sir, but neither is she . . ."

Magnus did not have to say anything more. Abdee immediately guessed what the relationship had been between Magnus and Anna Tyler. He asked, "What if her husband finds out? You know how white men feel about their women getting a taste of nigger prick?"

"Tyler's never around his wife that much to find out."

Emerging from the *sala de tormenta*, continuing down the torchlit hall toward a row of squat wooden doors, Abdee warned, "Black boy, you watch out, do you hear? I don't want some jealous American husband nutting my best nigger! They do things like that in Louisiana, you know."

"There's something about Mrs. Tyler I do have to warn you about, Master, Sir. She likes to talk a lot. She's good at asking questions."

Abdee grunted.

Magnus conintued, "She really likes asking questions about . . . you."

"Me?"

"Don't worry, Master Abdee, Sir. I didn't tell her

nothing. Not that I know much to tell about you, but I keeps my mouth right shut all the same."

Having always guarded his privacy against intruders, Abdee fumed at the idea of some inquisitive women trying to eke out information about him from one of his slaves.

He said, "Keep her mouth full of pecker, boy, so she won't ask more questions."

Shrugging his broad shoulders, Magnus grinned, "That ain't her tightest hole . . ."

Impatient now with talk about meddling white women, Abdee said, "Tell me about the Cuban. How has Soto been spending his time here?"

"Senor Soto is very polite," Magnus assured Abdee as they moved through the faint clouds of smoke streaming from the torches. "Soto's big around as a rum barrel, but he's got the best manners of all three. Nothing sissified about him like that Frenchman. No lilac colognes and lace hankies dangling from his sleeves. The only thing I can't understand about this Senor Soto guy is the way he likes his loving. You know how wenches always gabs and gossips together in the kitchen? Well, I heard a couple of nigger gals chewing the rag the other day, saying that this Cuban wants them to whip him on the ass with a belt or paddle. Beat him like he was nothing but a little . . . baby!"

Abdee shook his head with distaste. Sexual perversions did not interest him. Anyway, not stories about men who yearned to be mastered by a slave.

Preferring to hear about the castle, Abdee next asked Magnus about the livestock pens, the irrigation system which he had only recently devised for the vegetable plots, inquiring which of the female slaves had become pregnant, and if any wench had given birth to a sucker in his absence.

Following Abdee down the line of wooden doors, Magnus answered these questions and then began to explain new difficulties between the mulatto cook, Consuela, and the short but buxom Negress, Luma, whom Abdee had placed in charge of maintaining and cleaning both the inside of the castle and the harbor yard.

Magnus explained, "These visitors, the crews from their three ships and all, they makes a lot more extra work for Consuela. Extra cooking. Extra cleaning. More work all around. She don't complain but I noticed lately she's more irritable. She's fighting a lot more lately with Luma."

"Luma? Why?"

"There's jealousy between those two wenches. Jealousy over you."

Dismissing the idea as female insipidness, Abdee asked, "What about Luma? How's she working?"

Magnus shook his head. "You might have to think about a new job for Luma. It ain't that she sluffs her chores. She's good at organizing folks to work. She just don't have no eye for house cleaning. Those cleaning gals do what Luma tells them but Luma just don't see where to clean. She forgets to tell the wenches to scrub the floors, polish silver, shake the rugs. She'd rather play around in the yard with that whip you gives her. She loves that leather snake of hers."

"You tell Luma I want to see her here in the Barracoon tonight. I'll be staying down here while everybody's having supper."

Agreeing to pass on the message, Magnus assured Abdee, "That's one thing Luma never forgets, Master, Sir. Seeing you. That Luma gal could hardly bear it till you gets back home. She's been worried sick you'd find some new African wench to replace her as your number one gal here. She's right stuck on you."

As if Magnus had reminded him of an important fact, Abdee said more brightly, "There is one wench I found. Come on. Take a look at her."

Stopping in front of the last door in the smoke-filled hallway, Abdee lifted a ring of keys from his belt. As he inserted a key into the hole in the round-topped door, he said, "She's Ashanti. I separated her from the rest of the slaves. When you see her you'll understand why I'm keeping her for myself."

Pushing open the wooden door with a creak, Abdee took the flickering torch from Magnus's hand. He held it out in the darkness of the vaulted room and asked, "What do you think, boy?"

Magnus gaped into the stone cell. Despite the darkness in front of him, he saw the outline of a woman chained to the far wall. She was staring at him, beseeching him for help as one African to another. Magnus's heart quickened as he kept studying the woman. He momentarily forgot about Abdee's presence beside him, realizing that he was looking at the most beautiful woman he had ever seen.

At that moment, Abdee stepped alongside him and warned, "Keep away from her, boy. She's my wench."

Magnus kept staring at the shackled woman. He thought of the words which his former master in America used to say, the maxim of "smelling the perfume at the first sight of a rose." Was this the meaning of those words about losing your heart to someone at first sight?

Abdee's voice came louder. "I said, boy, don't get any ideas. I know a horny nigger when I see one and you're one horny nigger right now."

Magnus turned to Abdee. He saw a sudden bitterness in his eyes. He realized that Abdee was serious—and rightly so, Magnus thought . . . *except I ain't horny for what you want, you son-of-a-bitch!*

Lowering his head, Magnus mumbled, "You've got yourself a mighty good woman . . . this time, Master Sir." The words choked him. He felt ashamed of himself for being so subservient, hating his position as slave.

When Abdee continued speaking to him, giving instructions about the messages he wanted taken to both Luma and Anna Tyler, Magnus barely heard the words. His mind again was on the Ashanti woman.

* * *

Magnus no longer exuded the same confidence he had last shown to Anna Tyler in her bedroom. He had come from the Barracoon to tell her that she would not be meeting Richard Abdee in the dining-hall. He paid little heed to Anna's angry reaction to his announcement. He was still besotted with Kinga.

Standing with lowered head, Magnus apologized to Anna Tyler, "There's nothing I can do, Missus Tyler, Mam. I cannot make my master speak to you. Mayhap, you should talk with your husband if you think you're . . ."

"Hugh? Speak to Hugh?" Anna threw back her head and laughed. "Hugh Tyler is too interested in black sluts to remember that I exist!"

Magnus could not tell if Anna was jealous or contemptuous of her husband spending time with black girls. He shrugged helplessly. He had his own problems to worry about now. The image of the Ashanti woman was burned onto his brain.

Crossing the Aubusson carpet to Magnus, Anna grasped his hands and said, "You seem to be my only friend here."

Magnus was not interested in confessions. He pulled his hands away from her, beginning to shake his head.

"No, no," Anna protested, moving closer, "I want to be your friend. To help you. I might be able to give you a future away from this despicable place."

Magnus felt her body press closer against him and his mind became more confused. A few days ago he would have readily responded to this white woman's sexual provocations, her promises for assistance.

But Magnus was no longer interested in making love to a white woman. He could not stop thinking about the Ashanti woman, not able to obliterate his sudden rush of feelings for her.

Laying her head against the bleached cotton shirt straining against the width of Magnus's chest, Anna continued, "I realized something which few women would ever admit. I realized it after I last saw you. I realized it as I sat here for long hours, waiting for my husband to come and say a few words to me. Waiting for my host, at least, to send some sign that I was welcome here. Can you understand, Magnus, when I say that I do not really *like* white men at all? That I, in fact, despise them?" Looking up into his soft brown eyes, she confessed, "Black men hold the secret for my happiness."

Magnus had guessed long ago that Anna Tyler was a devious woman, a person not to be trusted. But he did not know if she was being truthful to him now or playing another one of her artful games.

Nevertheless, Anna's carefully chosen words affected him. She sounded miserable and alone. Magnus knew that he was guilty of being gullible, too forgiving, too kind sometimes, but . . .

He reluctantly lifted one arm, wrapping it around her shoulder, now feeling weak and frail to him.

Instantly responding to the thoughtful embrace, Anna closed her eyes and held her mouth up to his. She pressed her body closer until she could feel that she was arousing his masculinity, causing his penis to strain the tightness of his cotton breeches.

Then, quickly slipping free from Magnus's grasp, Anna next sank to her knees in front of him, her hands caressing the bulge inside the breeches.

Towering above her kneeling figure, Magnus watched as Anna tore at his wooden buttons, working her tongue hungrily in her open mouth, rubbing her breasts against his knees. He could not stop her now.

Having successfully worked the white breeches down to Magnus's thighs, Anna held his phallus in one hand and turned her head to catch their reflection in the cheval mirror. She watched herself in the mirror as she moved her open mouth toward him, wetting his crown with her darting tongue, enclosing her lips around the growing hardness.

And it was at that moment that Magnus closed his eyes, hating himself for being a slave, cursing Abdee for keeping black people in this bondage. Magnus wondered if he might be wise to listen to Anna's plan for helping him in the future.

*   *   *

Anna Tyler fought the image of Richard Abdee in her brain as she knelt on the floor and stretched her mouth around Magnus's hard maleness, convincing herself that she did *not* wish that she was gratifying Richard Abdee instead of this black man. That she now hated Abdee. That she could never be servile to a man who ignored her. Those dreams were gone. Finished. And slowly eradicating her recent fantasies of meeting Abdee, the virile man she had pictured in her mind, Anna concentrated on Magnus. She held his scrotum in one hand and gripped his penis near its thick root with the other. She told herself that this was the excitement she truly craved. Then, turning toward the mirror, she looked at the reflection of herself kneeling in front of Magnus. Her heart quickened. The sight excited her. She pulled back her head and, pressing Magnus's erect brown penis along the side of her ivory face, she rubbed it against her cheek, smelling the cleanliness of his tightly stretched skin now wet with her own saliva. Next, moving to take the full crown back into her open lips, Anna completely exorcized the fantasy she had once entertained in her mind for Abdee. She would use Abdee's slave for her lusts and, by using this slave, making promises to him, she might well seek revenge against the slave's master for so rudely ignoring her. Sexual fulfillment for Anna Tyler was the mental stimulation of revenge and power, a need which did not satisfy her body as much as her vindictive mind. She also recognized the fact that this new subservience to Magnus punished her for foolishly hoping to satisfy Richard Abdee. And that thought of Abdee again made her take Magnus deeper into her throat, tasting only the dull sweetness of the black slave's virility. She had not felt the same perverse excitement since her first days of marriage to Hugh Tyler, submitting herself to a rough-edged, backwoods yokel with the sexual equipment of a plow horse. But now her satisfaction came from a Negro. The thought that she and her husband had made their fortune from selling such Negroes into slavery further embellished her demented lust. She moved her mouth more quickly now, pulling at his phallus with both hands, working feverishly to extract his seed.

5

LUMA

The slave girl, Luma, squatted behind a table in a far corner of the kitchen tonight, waiting for the hour to arrive when she could creep down the winding staircase and meet her master in the Barracoon. She had received the message from Magnus that she was to leave the kitchen at the time that the serving girls began carrying the food trays to the dining-hall.

Watching the chubby cook, Consuela, storm across the kitchen, Luma squeezed the leather butt of the bullwhip she always carried around the castle. The mere feel of the whip gave her confidence. And as Consuela was in a vile temper tonight, Luma was glad she had a way to protect herself.

Luma wished that she could leave the kitchen at this very moment. Consuela was screaming at the two small black children, Moggy, a nine-year-old boy, and Lisa, a ten-year-old girl, who helped with the kitchen chores. Consuela bossed Moggy to keep the charcoal glowing in the hearth, nagging at Lisa to slow the rotations of the mutton leg sizzling on the iron spit, warning them both to keep their fingers out of the root vegetables stewing in brown earthen pots, threatening the children that she would chop up their fingers like carrots if they disobeyed her.

Ordinarily, Luma would not stay near Consuela when she was in one of these foul moods. Consuela had Spanish blood mixed with the African, a volatile combination which often erupted into ferocious temper tantrums.

Although rotund, Consuela was a pretty girl. Her black hair curled into short ringlets around her chubby face. Her eyes were round and flashing; she had long, sooty lashes, and a small bowed mouth—but tonight her cupid lips were pinched tight with hatred.

Luma did not know Consuela's exact age but guessed that she was only a few years older than herself, probably no more than twenty-three or -four years old. Abdee had bought her in San Juan only a few months before he had found Luma for sale in a dockside slaveyard in the seedy South American port of Maracaibo.

Luma and Consuela had begun life here as good friends, comparing their childhood in slavery, laughing at how they learned to find a way around lazy masters and mistresses. When Richard Abdee showed a sexual interest in Luma, though, Consuela's Spanish blood boiled with jealousy. Luma knew that Consuela was in love with Richard Abdee herself.

It was bad enough having Negro blood in your veins, Luma believed, but if a girl was fat, too, life did not go easy on her. Luma could not understand why Consuela did not set her goals on a man more attainable then Richard Abdee, not to aspire to such high stakes in love as someone as magnificent as their English master.

Hearing the doorway from the dining-hall open into the kitchen, Luma peeked around the corner of the starched white cloth hanging from the table.

Her heart began to race when she saw two Negresses wearing fresh white kerchiefs on their heads coming in to fetch the first course for dinner. They were Daisy and Eula, two wenches who had spent the last week pestering with the American slave dealer, Hugh Tyler.

Consuela spun around at the sound of the door. She also knew that the appearance of these serving girls was the cue for Luma to meet Richard Abdee in the Barracoon.

Grabbing her whip and quickly darting toward the door, Luma heard a loud shriek behind her. She looked over her shoulder and saw Consuela grabbing for a kitchen knife.

"Merde!" Consuela screamed, *"Vaya, Puta puerco! Vaya!"* She yanked the knife from the chopping block and raised it above the puffed shoulder straps of her long apron.

Before Luma could dash through the door, the knife sang past her ear, landing with a steely shudder in the wooden door jamb.

Luma had had enough! She pulled back the bullwhip, flailing its leather tip across the kitchen. Her aim was not good. The tip knocked over a cream jug sitting on the dairy table, splattering its contents down the side, forming a thick white pool of precious cream on the flagstone floor.

"Puta!" Consuela screamed, rushing for another knife. Eula, Daisy, and little Lisa and Moggy all rushed for cover behind high-backed chairs as Consuela screeched. *"Vaya, Puta de Maracaibo!"*

But quickly trailing the long whip behind her, Luma escaped through the door. She stood panting in the hallway between the kitchen and the dining-hall. She finally turned toward a third archway, disappearing down into the darkness of the stairway which led to the Barracoon, muttering to herself that someday she would learn to use the whip with the expertise of her master, that she would rip Consuella's dress right off her body with the whip, lashing the Spanish bitch until her fat body was crisscrossed with bloody lines.

*   *   *

The stone steps felt cool to Luma's tiny bare feet. She pattered deeper down the twisting stairway, soon hearing the raucous sounds of men's voices. She had reached the first landing of the dungeons, the level which housed the crews from visiting ships.

Luma did not like this section of the castle where the sailors lived. These men were evil, using women like waterfront whores. Luma felt extremely lucky not to be one of the wenches who had to serve food to these drunken bastards and having to stay to provide sexual pleasures for them as well. She hurried down the next winding circle of steps.

Reaching the bottom landing, Luma moved stealthily along a twisting hallway lit only with sputtering torches. This lowest section of the dungeon was tomb-like compared to the sailor's quarters. Luma hated it even more. The slaves brought from Africa lay locked here in chains, groaning and crying behind every wooden door which lined the shadowy hallway.

Quickly padding along the hall in her bare feet, Luma reached to smooth her hair. She had taken special care in preparing herself for this evening, having arranged her black hair away from her forehead, brushing it up from her small face like a great mane of finely spun wool. Luma did not have natural curls like Consuela, but, nevertheless, her hair was not kinky and unmanageable like so many Negresses'.

Also, Luma had used some white paint from a small milkglass pot which the American woman, Anna Tyler, had thrown away. Luma had dabbed the white paint on her eyelids to make them stand out from her coal black skin. Although her dress was nothing more than a common slave shift, she had artfully altered it with a pair of scissors, needle, and thread, and now the hem cut above her dimpled knees, the neckline plunged to show the cleavage of her over-ample breasts. Luma saw no reason to hide the parts of her body which most pleased her master . . . breasts, legs, the warmth in between.

Tapping on the last wooden door in the hallway as she had been instructed by Magnus to do, Luma dropped her whip to the stone floor. Abdee had given her the whip as a symbol of her authority in the yard but he did not like her carrying it in his presence.

Turning the iron ring, Luma slowly pushed open the thick door and slowly entered the small room. She saw a torch smoking on an iron bracket in one corner.

Adjusting her eyes to the flickering light, she next saw Abdee laying on a straw pallet against the far wall. Her heart began to beat when she saw him lift one hand to her. She heard him slur, "Don't be bashful. Come on . . . get over here."

Gently closing the heavy door behind her, Luma could already smell the sweet odor of rum intermingled with the pungent scent of straw in the small room. She knew that Abdee had been drinking. She remembered how rum often made him treat her like an animal. Yet she tried to smile, reminding herself that she was lucky to be chosen again by Master Abdee.

71

Letting Abdee pull her roughly down to him on the pallet, Luma smelled his foul breath. His body reeked of perspiration. His groping fingers hurt her arms.

Fleetingly, Luma remembered how much more magnificent Richard Abdee seemed in her private thoughts, that she always concentrated on his silky blond hair, his cornflower blue eyes, his muscle-hard body when she was away from him. But here in the Barracoon, he was only drunken, clumsy, thoughtless . . .

Stop it, Luma told herself. You must not feel disappointed in your master. It is an honor to be with him. He has travelled thousands of miles across the ocean and you are the first woman he has chosen.

Wasting no time with romantic foreplay, Abdee pressed Luma down to the pallet with one hand and yanked up the shift above her waist with the other. He voraciously lowered his mouth to her breasts, fingering the wetness between her legs as he said, "You're a hot little piece . . . look at these big tits . . ."

Instinctively spreading her short legs for Abdee's pleasure, Luma watched Abdee through half-closed eyes as he enjoyed her body. Then when he pulled back to lower his breeches, she struggled to pull the shift over her head. She wanted to allow him an easier grasp of her breasts yet, still, she did not want to rumple her hair.

Lying naked now on the straw pallet, Luma arched her back for Abdee, giving him total access to her breasts. She rubbed the flatness above her wiry patch with the tips of her tiny fingers, remembering what actions pleased her master's eyes, what squirms, groans, gyrations, made him appreciate her more.

Not kissing Luma, Abdee kept prodding her

breasts, pulling at her spreading nipples, his phallus now bobbing hard with excitement over her stomach. She kept pumping her hips, simulating groans of pleasure as he moved his phallus down between her legs.

Suddenly Luma gasped. She had seen a shape in the corner of the dungeon room, a shape which looked like an outline of a woman . . . yes, it was a black woman and she was . . . chained to a wall! Like a dog!

Raising herself onto her elbows, she whispered, "Who's that?"

"*Bitch!*" Abdee snarled, rearing back and slapping her across the face with the back of his hand. "Don't ask questions, bitch!"

Falling over Luma's slumped body, he jammed his now erect penis into her, continuing to call her derogatory names and proceeding to slap her against the buttocks, the legs, her breasts, even her face, even pulling at her thoughtfully arranged hair.

For the first time that she could remember, Luma felt ashamed to be subservient to her master. Was it because he was becoming more brutal and selfish than before? Or was it because another woman was watching, a black African woman chained to the wall? Luma wondered who the woman was, the reason Abdee had her here, if this was punishment for herself or—could it be—the shackled woman?

6

ABDEE SLAVES

The morning sun moved in a burst of gold toward the thin horizon; soon, the radiant smudge became a visible sphere, its brilliance coloring the sky and shimmering across the azure waters of the Caribbean, bathing the eastern walls of *Castelo Novo Mundo*.

As the sun inched higher, the castle cast a long westward shadow across the water as if it were a sundial gauging time on the flatness of the sea. And from the shadow moved the top-heavy outline of a ship, the morning winds catching its white unfurling sails . . . Captain Pennington was sailing the *Petit Jour* at daybreak for the island of Dominica.

Links of iron chain ground against one another on a windlass bedded inside the castle's hollow walls as the portcullis lowered after the ship's departure. Then, when that grating noise subsided, the castle was once again made impregnable, and, slowly, a growing cacophony of morning life began to rise from the many levels of courtyards, pens, and towers within the castellated tower.

The crow of a cockerel cut the sleepy stillness from a roof behind the northern wall. A pair of wooden shutters creaked open on a window high above the harbor. A black woman hummed a tune as she pushed out two fluffy white feather pillows for airing. A second pair of shutters opened with a clatter; another Negress began shaking dust from a rag carpet while the metallic echo of kettles clanked from the kitchen deep within the castle.

A wooden door swung open on leather hinges and the small kitchen girl, Lisa, emerged into the harbor yard. She wore a shapeless shift. Her feet were bare. Carrying a wicker basket over one skinny arm, Lisa lingered in the sloping dirt yard to look at the three ships still anchored in the harbor.

These ships came from a world outside *Castelo Novo Mundo*. The very young slaves like Lisa and Moggy who had been born here never saw that world beyond the ocean. They had only heard stories from older blacks who had been purchased in faraway ports with curious sounding names like Havana . . . Fort Royal . . . Maracaibo . . . Puerto Rico . . . New Orleans . . .

The children here only dreamt about magical lands where grass spread in open fields, where water ran in ribbons over speckled rocks, where fruit hung upon trees, where cows had pastures in which to graze instead of a small manger bounded on all sides with walls of bleak, cold stone.

Suddenly hearing the clank of leg irons echoing from behind an iron grille on the far side of the harbor, Lisa quickly scampered along the narrow dirt yard. She knew that the grille opened onto stairs which descended into the Barracoon. The clank of chains told Lisa that the new slaves were being brought up into the yard for their morning exercises.

Lisa had seen the black people unloaded from Master Abdee's ship yesterday. Consuela had told her that these new black people would not stay here for long. That they came from a faraway land called Africa. That they would soon be taken away to another distant place, maybe Havana . . . or Fort Royal . . . or New Orleans . . . and sold to white people even richer than Master Abdee.

Pulling the rope handle on another wooden door farther down the yard, Lisa disappeared up a long climb of steps to collect the morning's eggs. Consuela was waiting for them in the kitchen.

* * *

Richard Abdee drifted toward consciousness this morning with a single thought forming in his rum-dulled mind. Today he had to meet Tyler, Soto, and Saint-Barbot.

Coming further out of his sluggish sleep, he blinked at a shaft of sunlight cutting through a slit high above him on a stone wall. He remembered coming to this room in the sailor's barracks last night after satisfying himself with Luma.

Abdee also remembered Luma struggling to pull a rumpled shift over her tousled hair last night, how she had staggered from the cell in the Barracoon. He recalled an Ibo guard, too, leading Kinga from the room. Kinga had remained chained to the wall throughout his lovemaking with Luma. Abdee wondered how much Kinga had seen, what she had understood about his intentions . . .

Stretching his naked arms above his head, Abdee sniffed Luma's musty odor still clinging to his skin. His maleness throbbed with the morning firmness of a nineteen-year-old buck. He rolled over on his side, thinking how he would enjoy making love again this morning. But the image in his mind was not of Luma. He thought instead about Kinga. He ached more than ever to enjoy her in his bed.

But, having no time this morning to indulge his plans for training Kinga in the way he controlled Luma, Abdee threw back the muslin sheet and hopped out of the single cot. He remembered that he had told Magnus to meet him in the Barracoon and help make preparations for the dealers to inspect the slaves. Abdee knew that the quicker he sold the slaves for a good price and they were taken away from here, the sooner he could concentrate on Kinga . . . and searching for his own plantation.

While washing himself in cold water, shaving, and dressing in the fresh clothes waiting for him in a candlelit room deep below sea level, Abdee informed Magnus about the manner in which he would meet the three slave merchants this morning. That he wanted Magnus to escort Tyler, Soto, and Saint-Barbot to the Barracoon where he would let them have their first look in the cells.

Without his usual morning chatter, Magnus glumly turned away from Abdee to expedite his orders. He was unusually sober this morning. He knew that if he remained alone with Abdee too long he might ask him if he had made love to the Ashanti woman last night. Magnus knew better than to ask Abdee questions. He knew his master's ferocious temper, how enraged Abdee became when questions were asked about his privacy, especially about a woman he guarded so jealously.

When Magnus eventually reappeared in the Barracoon with Hugh Tyler, Claude Saint-Barbot, and Ignatio Soto, Abdee had finished dressing in the fresh clothing, his blond hair slicked back from his forehead with water, his brain cleared by gulping cups of strong black coffee.

Abdee kept his welcome brief, saying, "It is not customary for me to show any of my slaves here at the castle, gentlemen. But as you took so much trouble to come all this way, I am going to make this one concession."

Ignatio Soto stepped forward and nodded his head in a curt but polite bow, his pointed beard touched his pleated waistcoat. He spoke in a richly accented voice, "I have heard you were difficult, Senor Abdee. *Muy trabajoso*. And *egoísto*. Also, that you lead the private life of an *ermitano*. But I have been shown nothing but courtesy since my arrival at *Castelo Novo Mundo*. Let me take this opportunity now to thank you. It has been as if you had . . . expected us. Every facet of hospitality has been shown to me. *Gracias*, Senor."

Admiring the Cuban's directness, Abdee looked him in the eye and answered, "A businessman known for his wisdom and great wealth is always welcome here, Don Ignatio. My people have a list of which ships to allow into the harbor. I would flog any slave who did not welcome a prosperous man like you in my home."

Claude Saint-Barbot interrupted, asking in a cold thin voice, "Does that mean that only men of great riches are welcome at *Castelo Novo Mundo*?"

Studying the lean, exquisitely dressed Frenchman, Abdee said, "The master of *Côte Rouge* cannot be poor."

Saint-Barbot did not reply to Abdee's statement. Not a muscle moved in his sallow face; his long, thin moustache remained immobile; the curls of his European wig lay upon the shoulders of his brocade jacket as if they were hewn from honey-tinted marble.

Hugh Tyler had less polish than the Frenchman, less flair than the portly slave dealer from Havana. Although expensively attired in fine brown leather boots and a suit of thin beige wool, Tyler exuded the ruggedness of someone from a pioneer land. He had broad shoulders, a thickset chest, and sturdy legs. He wore no wig, his light brown hair cut short and parted to one side of his mild-featured face. Abdee could not tell if Hugh Tyler was an ignorant country bumpkin or a clever man hiding behind a veneer of unpolished, almost crude mannerisms.

He drawled to Abdee, "These niggers we'll be seeing this morning, are they all from this last trip you made to Africa, or are you mixing in some of your other slaves?"

"You'll be seeing four hundred and twenty-five blacks, Mister Tyler. All from the last voyage to Africa." As Abdee answered, he remembered Magnus's words about Hugh Tyler pestering with the slave girls here. He wondered what such a virile white man would do if he knew that a Negro buck was making love to his wife. What kind of life did Hugh and Anna Tyler have together? How closely was she involved in his business? Why had Tyler even brought the inquisitive woman with him here?

Claude Saint-Barbot spoke again. He said, "Monsieur Abdee, we know nothing about your sales technique. How long do you plan to take before conducting the auction for your—" he waved a square of Mechlin lace,"—new African slaves?"

"Gentlemen," Abdee said. "We are jumping to conclusions. Please, don't talk about auctions and buying before you've even had a chance to inspect the slaves."

Grabbing a pine torch from an iron ring on the wall, Abdee said, "Follow me. I'll give you your first look. If you see anything which pleases you, you can return separately to the Barracoon for a more thorough . . . a more private inspection."

Then, turning to Magnus, he ordered, "Run ahead, boy, and tell the guards to light the torches by all the pens."

* * *

The first cell had Negroes to be sold as field workers, hard-muscled black men standing or squatting on banks of straw inside the iron bars which lined the hall. Some Negroes turned to meet the white men's stares with sullen expressions, others looked nervously down to the leg irons clamped around their ankles.

Stepping toward the bars for a closer look into the low-ceilinged room, Soto said, "They seem healthy. But I need more than good health. On Cuban *fincas*, the planters also look for breeders." He turned and walked to the next cell.

It was too soon for Abdee to tell if Soto was impressed or not with what he saw. He spoke of breeding but had not asked to inspect the genitals of any Negro.

The next pen contained taller but more narrow-shouldered men. Also, their faces were flatter than the last Negroes. Abdee had purposely made this division among the blacks.

Looking into this next pen, Soto grunted, "Krus."

Abdee nodded at Soto's recognition of the tribe from which these flat-faced men came. He suspected that Soto probably knew a great deal about African blood.

Claude Saint-Barbot still had not commented on

any of the Negroes. He looked fleetingly into one cell and, walking ahead of Abdee, he tipped his head toward the next. He was the only man in the group who shivered in the coldness of the Barracoon, his pale hands frequently rubbing his arms for warmth.

Soon, Abdee led them toward a cell containing only female slaves. These women also sat and lounged on the straw-covered floor but, unlike the males, they looked pleadingly as the white men stared at them in the flickering torchlight.

Tyler showed his first enthusiasm, "Good wenches. Mighty good wenches from what I can tell from here."

Abdee offered, "Inspect one." He motioned for Magnus to unlock the pen with the ring of keys. Next, he pointed toward a young Negress, ordering an Ibo guard to bring her out into the hallway.

The girl soon stood quivering in the circle of white men, closing her eyes in terror as Hugh Tyler began to prod at her legs, squeeze her thighs and breasts, opening her mouth to inspect her teeth, studying the soles of her feet, then feeling between her legs for virginity.

Abdee said, "I haven't squeezed lemon juice into their vaginas yet to test for syphilis or I would offer you one of these wenches, Mister Tyler."

Shaking his head, Hugh Tyler removed his hands from the girl and shoved her back toward the guard. He complimented, "Fine stock, mighty fine stock."

Nodding for Magnus to take the Negress back into the pen, Abdee led the three men around a corner and down the next long hallway of the Barracoon.

Saint-Barbot finally asked a question, his voice echoing in the cavernous hallway as he called, "You say you have four hundred and twenty-five slaves for sale, Monsieur Abdee. How many are dams? How many are sires?"

"One hundred and ninety-five are wenches," Abdee answered. "Thirty of them are pregnant."

Tyler said, "You should have more wenches knocked up, Abdee. A knocked-up wench fetches a higher price in Louisiana."

Abdee answered over his shoulder, "Selling blacks in Louisiana is your problem, Mister Tyler. Not mine."

Then beckoning the three men to inspect a large pen with a double expanse of iron bars, Abdee explained, "These are mostly saplings. Children not fully grown."

He stood to one side as Magnus unlocked the gate and a guard moved inside the pen with his torch to show the children more closely. Some of the young girls had breasts barely bigger than buttons while others already protruded in full maturity. A few of the boys had penises no bigger than acorns but other boys had sexually matured far beyond their pubescent years.

Soto pointed toward a group of semi-naked youths grouped in a far corner of the pen, saying, "Those in the huddle over here. The tall ones. They look like Ashanti."

"You're right," Abdee assured him. "They are Ashanti. You see here a mixture of Ashanti, Kru, and Mundingo."

Tyler whistled. "This doesn't sound like it's going to be a cheap proposition. Ashanti and Mundingo stock. That costs money."

"Whatever you pay me, Mister Tyler, you'll more than recoup in New Orleans."

"How exactly do you mean to auction these?" Tyler asked. "Are you going to sell them singly or by chains of, say, ten niggers to a coffle?"

"I'm going to sell them in any way or manner I can, Mister Tyler, to any man who offers me the most money."

Soto folded his arms across the gold chains festooning his brocade waistcoat, saying "To hold an ordinary sale—to sell the slaves one by one—that would take too long. I do not know about these two gentlemen here but, as for myself, I must return to Havana for urgent business. I personally would prefer an auction of larger groups. Even groups of ten is too small for four hundred and twenty-five slaves."

Saint-Barbot quickly said, "But if they are sold in large groups the prices will certainly rise too fast."

Hugh Tyler disagreed, "I think Soto's idea for a group auction is damned good. Hell, I've seen enough to offer a bid right now. In one big lot."

Soto and Saint-Barbot stared at Tyler. Was this American crazy? Abdee had not shown them more than twelve or fourteen cells. There may be at least a hundred slaves yet to see, not to mention, examine more closely.

Saint-Barbot said disdainfully, "I have never heard such nonsense. Buying so many slaves in one . . . lot."

Stroking his pointed beard, Ignatio Soto said, "Mister Tyler must have more money than we do, Monsieur Saint-Barbot."

Ignoring the two men, Tyler put his arm around the shoulder of Abdee's nankeen shirt, saying, "I'm willing to give you a bid for all four hundred and twenty-five niggers right now. On the strength of what I've just seen."

Although the idea intrigued Abdee, he hated to be rushed. He said, "I suggest that you three gentlemen examine each and every nigger carefully before you make any commitments."

Then, turning to Magnus, Abdee said, "Go upstairs. Tell Consuela that I'll be joining everyone for the midday meal. Perhaps these gentlemen will have reached some decision by that time."

Feeling more optimistic about his future than he had in a long time, Abdee thought of fertile soil, of Kinga, of life on a rich plantation, sharing a home once again with a devastating black woman, rebuilding a life he had once known on Dragonard Plantation.

*   *   *

Anna was right after all, Hugh Tyler decided as he wandered alone now in the passageway lined by iron-barred cells, waiting for the first group of slaves to be taken into one large room. His wife had told him that Abdee's slaves were always prime. She had promised him that the journey here would not be a waste of time. He did not even have to see more niggers to know that they would average two thousand dollars per head on the auction block—and that was a low estimate.

Anna had also predicted that the United States of America government was on the verge of buying a vast tract of land from France called the Louisiana Territory. As soon as President Thomas Jefferson finalized that purchase, the Napoleanic embargo would be lifted from the New Orelans harbor. Ships could sail again to the cloth mills in Manchester, England. American cotton prices would soar. The demand for slaves would go wild in Louisiana. No, Hugh Tyler knew that he would not lose on whatever price he bid for the four hundred and twenty-five Abdee slaves.

Waiting now for the guards to lead the slaves into

the room for a closer inspection, Tyler decided that his only remaining problem was Anna herself. She had almost been acting in outright contempt for him. Why is she staying away from me so much, he wondered? Why is she not trying to persuade me to sleep with her? All I need is some coaxing, a little sign that she still loves me!

If Hugh Tyler did not know that his wife had a distaste for love making, he would suspect that she was having an illicit affair with another man. It was not natural for a woman to allow her husband to amuse himself with so many black wenches. Didn't Anna ever get jealous? One mere show of affection from her and he would be back in her bed in a minute.

Their last few years of marriage had been strained. Anna seemed to thrive on reminding him about his dependancy on her family money. How she owned the Tyler Auction House. Not him. That he was nothing more than her puppet. But he was used to that.

What bothered him was when his wife blamed her distaste for sex on what she called his "clumsy love-making." Anna deeply hurt him when she accused him of being nothing but a big, clumsy, dumb farmboy.

Dumb! Hugh Tyler hated to be called dumb! He realized that he was not sophisticated, suave, or debonair. But, hell, the only debonair men in a town like New Orleans were either perverts or dandies with nigger blood in their veins!

Hugh Tyler tried to convince himself this morning in the Barracoon that Anna was acting strangely because she was frightened—scared to death about being marooned here on this island castle with nothing but water—and stinking niggers—all around her.

At that moment, Magnus approached Hugh Tyler, politely informing him that the slaves were ready to be examined. Hugh Tyler had noticed in the last few days that Magnus was a very impressive, virile, young buck. He wished that he could buy him, too. He would like to take a good, smart nigger like Magnus back to New Orleans. He made a mental note to mention the fact to Anna. They had talked this morning about the limit he should bid for all four hundred and twenty-five Abdee slaves. He doubted if she would be too excited, though, about offering Abdee a price for Magnus. Hugh Tyler knew that his wife disliked educated blacks.

7

A HARBOR FIRE

The announcement in the kitchen this morning that Richard Abdee would be joining his guests in the dining-hall for the midday meal threw Consuela into a panic. She had not planned to prepare anything particularly special for today's repast but, now, hearing that Abdee finally would be emerging from the Barracoon, Consuela set about to serve a feast which would ordinarily take days to prepare.

First, she dispatched Lisa, the kitchen girl, to find Lolly Mumba and tell her to wring the necks of six plump hens while she sent another child up to the supply room in a turret to bring down a smoked ham, plus a string of cheeses which she kept there in jars of vinegar.

At the same time, Consuela hurried Moggy to fan the coals in the kitchen hearth. She would boil tomatoes and then mash them into a pulp, chilling the blood-red liquid in a deep cistern to make a spicy Andalusian soup called *gazpacho*.

Also, Consuela decided to forgo the Peruvian wine she had been serving to the guests since their arrival at *Castelo Novo Mundo*. She asked Magnus to take his key for the liquor cellars and fetch the finest Castegna wine they kept in stock, plus a bottle of rum which she would use in a thick syrup for the almond cakes she was baking for the sweet course.

Long before Abdee emerged from the Barracoon, the massive oak table in the dining-hall glittered with silver cutlery and handwrought goblets. The plum-color damask curtains were thrown back from the tall, narrow windows and the bright Caribbean sun streamed down onto the richly-dyed Turkish carpets strewn in layers across the stone floor.

As no flowers grew at *Castelo Novo Mundo*, Consuela ordered Moggy and Lisa to fill the silver epergnes with greenery from the wisteria vines growing up the walls of the kitchen terrace. To these arrangements, she added feathers, stalks of dried wheat, brittle cornflowers, decorations which she kept stored in cotton bags hanging from the rafters in anticipation for some splendid banquet.

The result was beautiful—the epergnes towered with the muted colors at both ends of the table; the golden Sevres china glittered in front of each armed walnut chair; the sunlight danced in the opulent array of chased silver forks, knives, spoons, and goblets.

Taking a moment to survey her work, Consuela held her small hands to her breasts in pride. The Portugese castle had many treasures but Consuela rarely found time to use them. She felt at this moment as if *Castelo Novo Mundo* were a place to be proud of, not some shadowy, sinister slave market miles from nowhere.

Suddenly hearing the sound of footsteps behind her, she hurried to the arched doorway leading to the kitchen. She did not want Abdee to find her here. Consuela also had another plan, a plot which involved her love for Master Abdee.

Consuela had seen the bruises and scars on Luma this morning and rightly suspected that they had been inflicted on her last night by Master Abdee in the Barracoon. Consuela interpreted the bruises as proof that Luma had finally fallen from favor with Master Abdee. That he had beaten her out of . . . disgust. Consuela had no notions about sadistic love making.

In her misevaluation of Abdee's and Luma's sexual relationship, Consuela foresaw that the time had come for Abdee's attentions to turn to her. She had been telling herself all morning that it was up to her to act now, to make herself more physically attractive, to win—and keep—Abdee's devotion. The plan was to accelerate a diet she had already begun.

Although her cumbersome clothes concealed her body, not showing that she had already lost much weight, she decided to force herself to lose even more poundage. To make a visible difference. And fast. She would begin a very special diet in which she could gain nourishment and strength from food to perform the tasks with which Master Abdee had entrusted her and still lose pounds of excess fat at the same time.

As Consuela waddled from the dining-hall, her mind filled with the details about her strategy of winning Abdee's love, she suddenly noticed a tall figure lingering in the passageway between the dining-hall and the kitchen. It was the Frenchman! What was he doing here, using the back stairs which led to the sailors quarters and the Barracoon?

Claude Saint-Barbot looked startled at first, as if Consuela had surprised him sneaking up these back stairs. He was breathing very fast, too, as if he had been taking three steps at a time.

Grabbing the skirt of her long white apron, Consuela nodded her curly head at him and quickly curtsied in due respect.

Saint-Barbot stood staring at her. His thin lips suddenly lifted into a flashing smile and, as he gallantly returned Consuela's greeting, he murmured, "*Bonjour, Mademoiselle!*"

Mademoiselle! Consuela's heart reeled. No white man of any nationality had ever addressed her with such polished manners! And that smile! He was smiling at her. Do you think . . . ?

No, she told herself. How could an elegantly dressed handsome gentleman like Monsieur Saint-Barbot from Martinique ever be interested in the likes of her? But rushing red-faced into the kitchen, Consuela realized a frightening fact.

Am I really so much in love with Master Abdee? If a smile from someone as handsome as the Frenchman makes my heart flutter, then I certainly cannot be very serious about . . . . .

Aya! she thought, standing now with her back to the kitchen door. *Aya!* Lose some fat first, *puerco*, before you start picking and choosing who all your dashing lovers are going to be!

❋   ❋   ❋

Claude Saint-Barbot paused on the stairway after Consuela dashed into the kitchen, the palms of his hands covered with a nervous wetness. He had not expected such complications at *Castelo Novo Mundo*.

Saint-Barbot possessed neither the money nor the credit to make an offer for all the Abdee slaves. He had not planned to buy more than fifty blacks and resell them for a profit on Martinique. But now Hugh

Tyler had spoiled those ambitions. Nevertheless, Saint-Barbot knew that he could not leave here without anything, at least not without a plan which would somehow insure money for him in the near future.

Although Saint-Barbot's estate on Martinique, *Côte Rouge*, was heavily mortgaged, he had kept this fact a secret, even from his wife. He was glad now that Maxine was not able to travel, that she had not accompanied him to *Castelo Novo Mundo*.

Thinking about his wife, Saint-Barbot remembered the Spanish slave girl, Consuela, and he smiled at his new ploy to use her to secure his future. He knew to what lengths a female would go to obtain attention. His wife had taught him every dark corner of a woman's desirous mind.

Continuing up the back stairs to his quarters, Saint-Barbot thanked the Lord for making him a man who was not lustful for sexual fulfillment with either women or men, that his desires were only for physical comforts. He knew females were attracted to him, though, and if he laid his plans well in the next few hours, he could not only obtain the few slaves he wanted without paying any money for them, but also provide a financial security for himself and his wife, Maxine.

Saint-Barbot suspected that Maxine would certainly applaud his cunning, at least the less violent aspect of what he now planned. He would try to keep her from ever learning the more ruthless details which he had only a few minutes earlier finished discussing with his crew. Claude Saint-Barbot protected his wife as she in her special way protected him.

* * *

Abdee presided at the head of the table, dressed in the same boots, breeches, and open-necked nankeen shirt which he had put on hours ago this morning in the Barracoon. The only visible difference in him now was his mood—he looked confident, relaxed, almost reckless as he sat with one leg over the arm of his carved chair. He was richer now than he had been a few hours earlier; or, at least, he could be richer if he accepted the offer which Hugh Tyler had made for all four hundred and twenty-five slaves.

Senor Soto sat to Abdee's left, with Claude Saint-Barbot seated to the left of him. They showed none of Abdee's ebullience, they looked grim-faced down at the royal blue and gold plates setting in front of them on the table.

Across from Ignatio Soto, Anna Tyler was placed on Abdee's right, Hugh Tyler seated on the next chair—across from Claude Saint-Barbot. Tyler's good mood did not surprise Abdee, but his wife's sarcastic mood confused him. Dismissing the icy reception which Anna Tyler had given him when they had been introduced, Abdee mischievously awaited the change in her haughty expression when she saw the surprise he had in store for her. Abdee had invited Magnus to join them for coffee at the conclusion of the meal.

Table conversation began with indirect references to the near fortune which Tyler had offered Abdee only moments ago for the entire shipment of slaves, a bid which Abdee had provisionally accepted in the Barracoon.

Both Saint-Barbot and Soto knew that the amount was substantial, but neither had argued to top it. Nor were either the Cuban or the Frenchman willing to buy the entire consignment of slaves themselves, especially not without a much more thorough examination of the four hundred and twenty-five slaves than that which could be accomplished in a few short hours.

Wanting to keep the table conversation off the subject of slaves for the duration of the meal, Abdee said, "Mrs. Tyler would certainly be bored with conversation about business." He looked again at Anna Tyler and, appraising her cool manner, he decided that she was the kind of white woman who would not show a flicker of recognition toward Magnus when he finally arrived at the table. Abdee imagined her using any man, despite his color, according to her selfish whims.

Anna Tyler unexpectedly responded to Abdee's harmless statement. She said in a testy voice, "Don't be frightened of offending me, Mister Abdee. My husband and I discussed the offer at great length, before he even saw the slaves."

"You have such faith in my Negro stock?" Abdee asked, his blue eyes twinkling. The promise of money had made him jubilant. He would soon again have the means to afford his gnawing ambition, to stop dealing with slave merchants and isolate himself on acres of fertile ground, to have a slave village to sow, build, forge his every need.

Hugh Tyler leaned back in his chair, bragging, "My wife here might strike you as a retiring little lady, Mister Abdee, but Annie's one of the shrewdest slave dealers in all Louisiana."

Abdee nodded his head, noticing Anna Tyler wince at the sound of her husband's grating voice, his boasting about such a markedly unfeminine activity. Abdee had no doubt about the woman's shrewdness as a businesswoman. He wondered now about her attractiveness as a female. What about her excited Magnus? What was Anna Tyler like at lovemaking? Abdee thought, not too good.

The door from the kitchen then pushed open, Saint-Barbot jerked his head and looked anxiously toward it. His face sobered when he saw the two black serving girls, Eula and Daisy, entering with a tureen and bowls for the first course. Who had Saint-Barbot been expecting to see, Abdee wondered?

As the two girls proceeded to serve the chilled *gazpacho*, Hugh Tyler kept his eyes away from them, glancing nervously at his wife several times to see if she were studying him—or perhaps glaring at the two wenches who had been his habitual bedmates.

Looking at Saint-Barbot, Tyler awkwardly tried to initiate a conversation. He asked, "What would you get for a plantation like yours, Saint-Barbot?"

" 'Get'," Saint-Barbot repeated, reaching for his stemmed wine goblet. "I do not understand this 'get'?"

"If you had to sell it," Tyler explained, anxiously glaring at the girls making their rounds with the silver soup tureen and then back to Saint-Barbot.

"Sell?" asked Saint-Barbot. "I do not have to 'sell' *Côte Rouge!*"

Abdee listened avidly. The subject of Tyler's blundering diversion was just the question he himself would like to ask Saint-Barbot. But he knew better than to ask it now, especially at a moment when he knew that Saint-Barbot's pride was suffering from having been outbid for the slaves which he so badly wanted. Abdee had planned to make enquiries about *Côte Rouge* himself but in a more circuitous way, a more devious method befitting his nature.

Tyler drawled, "I don't mean no offence understand, I'm only asking, say, if you were to sell that place of yours on Martinique, what kind of price would you get for a tract like that?"

Saint-Barbot's answer was clipped. "I have no idea."

Ignatio Soto's mood had also been mysterious since leaving the Barracoon. Abdee did not know if he were angry, jealous or only annoyed that Tyler had preempted him with such a lavish bid. He knew that the Cuban had spoken resentfully about the amount of time this trip had cost him, time which could be spent looking after his interests in Havana.

Soto said, "I do not know about French colonies, but I hear that property on English islands like Jamaica or St. Thomas is very high. They are like Spanish holdings in Cuba. Although our governments are warring, property prices hold strong."

Turning to Abdee, Soto's face remained impassive as he continued, "the interesting fact is the price our host here paid for his Portuguese . . . tower."

Abdee glibly replied, "Who said I bought it?"

The jewels on Soto's hirsute fingers sparkled as he gestured to the opulent furnishings in the dining-hall. "But certainly it was no charter from the English government!"

Abdee admitted, "I am my own government." He did not want this conversation to get out of control. He preferred to listen more about land prices on Martinique than to explain how, when, or why he came to control *Castelo Novo Mundo*.

A smile crossing her thin mouth, Anna Tyler said, "*Castelo Novo Mundo* is like Tortuga then, Mister Abdee. You are answerable to no one?"

"Tortuga has been French for more than a hundred years," Abdee replied, suspecting what this suspicious American woman was trying to imply.

"French, perhaps . . . in name. But everyone knows that Tortuga has been the pawn of privateers since time *in memoriam*."

"Are you asking, Mrs. Tyler, if I'm a pirate?"

"A pirate?" Anna threw back her head and laughed. Then, snatching for an ivory-sided fan lying beside her plate, she flicked it open with a snap and began to flutter the pleated silk around her throat. "'Pirate' is a colloquialism for robber. I said 'privateers,' Mister Abdee. Men who wage war against foreign vessels for their sovereign. And *Castelo Novo Mundo* is most strategically placed for such activities. I am certain that King George would probably grant you no less than a peerage for such services. You certainly remember how the notorious Captain Morgan became governor of Jamaica?"

Abdee's good humor had completely disappeared. He did not want to talk about English government or royal favors to privateers. Nor did he want this inquisitive woman to learn his past included an English title. She would never stop asking questions then; she would want to know every detail of how he had long ago renounced his title of the Earl of Wycliffe.

He sharply answered, "I am not involved, nor have I ever been involved with government activities, Mrs. Tyler."

She still pursued, "But I heard a different story, Mister Abdee. I actually heard someone say in New Orleans that you once held a government post on the island of . . . where was it . . . St. Kitts?"

Hugh Tyler coughed nervously. Soto's finger smeared the moisture which the chilled white wine caused on his silver goblet. Claude Saint-Barbot glanced expectantly toward the kitchen door. The conversation was now a duel between Abdee and Anna Tyler, a battle for past facts and dubious professions.

"The only post I ever held on St. Kitts," Abdee answered coldly, "was one the English prefer to forget."

"The Dragonard!" Anna exclaimed, closing her fan with a snap. "That was it. The Dragonard! The public whipmaster in Basseterre! Yes, I'm beginning to remember more details now."

Ignatio Soto interrupted, "Like England, Spain has public whips in her colonies, too. But England has abandoned the practice of public whips on all her islands. As Mister Abdee says, they prefer to forget about them."

"Barbaric," Saint-Barbot muttered with feigned interest, his eyes again straying to the kitchen door. "Public whips . . . *tres grossier!*"

Soto mildly continued, "The problem of disciplining slaves has always been a difficult one in the West Indian colonies. A problem impossible to avoid. That is, except in a location such as this. I suspect that Mister Abdee's isolated location here in the Windward Islands prevents his slaves from ever escaping. I would doubt if there is any problem of discipline here at *Castelo Novo Mundo.*"

The door to the kitchen opened again and, first, Eula and Daisy entered to clear away the bowls, followed by Consuela carrying a large platter heaped with brown rice and dotted with chicken breasts baked with thinly sliced ham and melted cheese.

Saint-Barbot leapt to his feet, his sobriety quickly transforming into gallantry.

Anna Tyler looked quickly toward her husband, puzzled at the Frenchman standing for a servant girl—especially someone so fat and undistinguished as the half-caste cook, Consuela.

"*Mademoiselle,*" Saint-Barbot said, bowing as Consuela stood dumbstruck, holding the platter heaped with rice and garnished chicken. The Frenchman's earlier show of interest made Consuela change her vow of not allowing Master Abdee to see her until she had lost some weight. But standing now face to face with the impeccably attired Frenchman, seeing him pay all this attention to her, Consuela suddenly became awkward. She lost all confidence.

Although Abdee looked less attractive to her now, she looked toward the head of the table, saying, "This is the first meal I cook for my Master . . . since he return from Africa . . . welcome home . . . Master Abdee."

Settling himself in his chair again, Saint-Barbot said in enthusiasm which surprised the other guests, "You are a very lucky man, Monsieur Abdee. You have such . . . devotion here." Saint-Barbot's eyes followed Consuela around the table as he spoke. There was no doubt that he was smitten with her—or at least trying to show that he was.

Abdee realized at that moment that he had heard very little about Saint-Barbot's personal life, not knowing if he was married, or even betrothed.

He began. "I cannot imagine you having less devotion from your people on Martinique, Saint-Barbot . . ."

Stopping, Abdee whiffed a scent he knew was not from the aromatic spices garnishing the chicken. He also thought he heard an unusual amount of noise arising from below the windows in the dining-hall.

Consuela was standing by Saint-Barbot's chair. She nervously held the platter toward him, trying to avoid his eyes, wondering if she had been too brazen by bringing the main course into the dining-hall. Yet she had to see if the Frenchman's attention had been more than a pleasantry . . . and indeed it was!

Anna Tyler then turned to her husband and asked the question, "Do you smell something . . . burning?"

Sniffing, Hugh Tyler nodded that he did. And while Saint-Barbot was still smiling at Consuela, ignoring the Tylers' report that they smelled fire, Magnus burst into the dining-hall, breathlessly shouting, "Master Abdee, Sir! Master Abdee! The brig's on fire! The *Southern Zephyr*!"

100

Everything then happened so fast that Consuela could not remember later if the Frenchman had patted her wrist during the announcement—or only moments shortly after it—and whispered, *"You must not forget me, cherie. I shall return here like a gentleman."*

* * *

Clouds of black smoke billowed from the hatch of the *Southern Zephyr* when Abdee and Magnus reached the harbor. At the same moment, Ignatio Soto and Claude Saint-Barbot were rushing down the back stairs from the dining-hall to organize their separate crews for towing their own ships from the harbor, and Tyler raced to form his men into a bucket brigade, in an attempt to save his brigantine.

Anna Tyler had followed Abdee and Magnus from the dining-hall, pausing dumbstruck now in the main doorway of the castle, gasping at the flames already crackling up the masts and spreading toward the booms and wooden spars.

Gathering the skirts of her topaz dress in one hand, she ran down the steps, shouting to Abdee, "Send men aboard! You must fight it from the deck!"

Abdee ignored her maddening orders, thinking instead about the nature of this fire. He suspected it had not begun by accident. The flames travelled too quickly up the cordages, smoke flooding too profusely from the coaming which surrounded the hatch. He could only guess that the hull had been greased with lard and a torch set to it.

"Don't just stand there," Anna shrilled. "Send niggers aboard! Use blankets! Water! Anything! You've got to extinguish those flames!"

"Tell your husband to send your own crew . . . ,"

101

Abdee said, thinking who in the castle would start such a fire. Was this the work of jealousy?

As the sound of footsteps across the yard attracted his attention, Abdee saw that Ignatio Soto had shed his emerald velvet coat, and was leading his crew toward his ship, the *Casa d' Oro*, shouting to the sailors in Spanish to weigh anchor, to lower the long boats, and tow the *Casa d' Oro* through the gates and out to sea.

Claude Saint-Barbot and his white-shirted crew followed closely behind the Cuban sailors. Abdee noticed that Saint-Barbot had not only remained attired in the resplendent clothes which he had worn in the dining-hall but, also, that he had found time to select a wide-brimmed courtier's hat decorated with egrettes.

The long boats from Saint-Barbot's ship, the *Angelique*, splashed into the water. The windlass creaked. The chains rattled to weigh anchor. The sailors worked without a single order being shouted to them. Two boats of surly men bent over the oars of the *Angelique*'s long boats, pulling the ship toward the open portcullis.

Surprised to see the French hands already swarming the rigging, Abdee called to Saint-Barbot, "Keep your sails rolled! The winds are strong out there! Don't open sail!"

His words went unheeded. The *Casa d' Oro* moved between Abdee and the *Angelique*, cries in Spanish obliterating his warning to the Frenchman.

Also, by this time, Tyler's sailors swarmed into the yard with wooden buckets, falling into lines around the *Southern Zephyr*, passing water from the harbor along a quickly organized chain of men.

The larboard side of the *Southern Zephyr* was now a complete wall of flame; the mizzenmast, a fiery pike, and the rolled canvasses breaking into yellow bursts.

The smell of smoke and the din caused by shouting seamen brought Abdee's people in droves from every nook and pen of the castle. Although holding their hands to protect their faces from the heat, they crowded toward the harbor to secure a closer look at the burning ship.

Fearing a mast or beam might soon topple down, engulfing his people in flames, Abdee cursed the blacks to take refuge in the castle. He knew at that moment that the safest course of action would be to tow the *Southern Zephyr* out to sea. The brigantine could burn its toll there.

Nevertheless, it was too soon to suggest this. The flames could easily ignite the wooden beams of the portcullis if the burning ship were towed through the entrance. Abdee saw that Tyler had also though of such an action—he was shouting for men to climb the stern, barking at them to hoist anchor.

"Don't move it yet!" Abdee called.

Then, seeing Tyler rush to take the lead position in the bucket line, Abdee peeled off his own shirt and rushed up the gangplank to take the place behind him, repeating his fears of moving the burning ship under his gate.

Suddenly, Abdee heard a loud crack in the overhead fire. Ropes of flame fell from the spars to the deck, followed by a roll of burning canvas searing through the air. He pushed back Tyler just as the upper half of the mainmast thundered down toward the quarter deck.

The men in the bucket brigade fell back from the smoke driven out of the bulwark by the careening mast. Sparks and burning particles showered the harbor yard.

Tyler lay soot-faced next to Abdee at the base of the gangplank. Looking toward a belch of flame lashing from the starboard, he said with dazed eyes, "We lost her . . ."

Abdee was still more concerned now about his harbor. He saw that although the *Southern Zephyr* was entirely engulfed with flames, the fire had not yet reached its prow and ornately carved figurehead of a female personification of a zephyr.

Pointing toward the prow, Abdee shouted to Tyler over the confusion of voices, "A tow line can be tied around the figurehead . . . boats can drag her out to sea . . . the mast's fallen. There's no danger of fire now spreading to my gate . . ."

Tyler nodded his head. He muttered in defeat, "Go ahead."

Acting on that approval, Abdee beckoned Magnus toward him and waved for his work gangs to man three harbor shallops.

Anna Tyler rushed hysterically forward, shrieking, "What in God's name are you doing, Hugh? What is this tyrant making you do?"

Tyler's eyes remained fixed on the flaming wreckage. He murmured, "The only thing left to do . . . tow her out to sea . . ."

"Hugh Tyler, don't be weak! At least try to save the hull! We can rebuild her! Think of the money! Think of the slaves! How are we going to get them to New Orleans?"

"Anna, there's no use. Everything's gone . . . or going . . . just going all to hell."

At the sound of a splash, they both turned and saw Magnus's half naked body dive into the water and begin to take long strides toward the prow. The shallops were already forming between the ship and the castle's gateway.

Holding a rope in one hand, Magnus climbed up the curvature of the prow, quickly securing the rope around the carved figurehead, and dove back into the water again.

Abdee whistled orders for the men to heave, and, slowly, the three groups of Negro slaves began to pull, tugging the *Southern Zephyr* toward the gate.

Standing soberly alongside his wife in the yard, Tyler watched the ship being dragged toward the entrance as Abdee approached them.

Without taking his eyes from the flaming spectacle, he said to Abdee, "I've got a confession to make to you."

Abdee was not listening. Another sight had caught his eye.

Tyler continued in a wavering voice, "I thought at first that you set this fire. But—" he shook his head "—no man would have worked like you. Or risked his nigger's lives . . ."

Abdee still stared beyond the brigantine, burning now outside the harbor, studying the full sails of another ship beyond, a vessel whose sails were already catching a wind from the open sea.

As Tyler also saw the other ship sailing away from *Castelo Novo Mundo,* he yelled, "Look! The Frenchman! That son-of-a-bitch is leaving!"

Abdee soberly nodded, but checked himself of accusing Saint-Barbot of setting fire to the *Southern Zephyr.* Could any man be so vindictive to commit arson because someone else had bettered him in a competition for four hundred and twenty-five slaves? Abdee immediately answered yes, a man could be that vindictive. He knew that he himself could. He even knew that he would do worse to Saint-Barbot if the destruction of the *Southern Zephyr* meant a cancellation of Tyler's offer to buy the slaves.

8

THE GOLDEN WIRES

Captain Pennington returned from Portsmouth early the following morning according to command, reporting to Abdee that he had sighted the *Angelique* giving wide berth to Barbados on a northwest course.

Abdee received Pennington in the dining-hall, eating his breakfast at the end of the long oak table. Another setting had been laid to his right, but, not inviting Pennington to sit down, he listened quietly as Pennington explained that he had, at first, thought that the *Angelique* was a Dutch frigate travelling toward Dominica. That he had chosen not to become entangled with one of the many Dutch warships now cruising the Caribbean, that the *Angelique* sailed alee before he caught her guidon in his spyglass.

Seeing the futility of castigating Pennington for this awkwardness, Abdee briefly recounted yesterday's events of the *Southern Zephyr*'s burning in the harbor and Saint-Barbot's sudden mysterious departure.

Next, he proceeded to order Pennington to be prepared to sail to New Orleans at short notice. Possibly tomorrow's dawn. Hugh Tyler had offered to rent the services of the *Petit Jour* and its crew to transport four hundred and twenty-five slaves to Louisiana. Tyler and Abdee had exchanged a written agreement; Abdee, selling Tyler the slaves; Tyler giving Abdee a banker's draft payable on their collection in New Orleans.

Dismissing Captain Pennington with orders to unload the supplies immediately from the *Petit Jour*, Abdee remained seated at the table, reviewing the situation in which he suddenly found himself. Yesterday's fire had altered his own future plans as drastically as it had done for the Tylers.

First, Abdee remembered his agreement with the African caboceer, "Store Man," to return to Port Weston before the rainy season and collect three hundred new prisoners, to be taken by the Ibo Tribe. He somehow had to find a way to accomplish that, arriving at the slave coast in time to purchase two hundred additional slaves to fill a tightly packed ship.

Unfortunately, Abdee's need for money was too great not to accept Hugh Tyler's offer of an extra five thousand dollars to transport the slaves to New Orleans. He needed every possible bit of money to reestablish himself on a plantation. His dream was to keep *Castelo Novo Mundo,* foreseeing this castle as becoming a breeding island.

Then came the problem of Kinga. Although he wanted to keep his slave stock fresh at the castle with the Negroes he had withheld from the sale, he did not want another man mating with Kinga. He somehow had to keep her untouched.

The only man who might possibly try to help Kinga would be Magnus. Abdee remembered Magnus's stunned silence when he had first seen Kinga in the cell. He had known then that Magnus might become a threat to him. It would be foolish to leave a man smitten like Magnus alone here with Kinga. Yes, Abdee decided, he would take Magnus with him to New Orleans.

Considering how he could be doubly sure that Kinga remained chaste in his absence, Abdee thought of the Ashanti craftsman, Pra. He remembered how he had not wanted to buy Pra from "Store Man." That he had almost whipped Pra to death for trying to smash Kinga's skull in the hold of the ship. Perhaps he could finally get some use from that sinister looking African.

Pra hated Kinga. Abdee knew that this hatred was deeply rooted in their past. Also, Pra was adept at using needles and blades. And thinking of a special bondage for Kinga, Abdee suspected that he would not even have to order Pra to affix it to her. He decided then to have Pra taken from his isolated cell and taken to the *sala de tormenta*. Abdee would meet him—and Kinga—there after he talked with Ignatio Soto.

* * *

Ignatio Soto joined Abdee a short time later in the dining-hall, sitting at the place set to Abdee's left. He showed no curiosity about this early morning invitation to discuss some future business venture between himself and Abdee.

Abdee began, "You haven't come up with a bid to top Mister Tyler's. So, I'm accepting his. Also, I will be taking the blacks to New Orleans myself. I have another proposition to discuss with you."

Soto remained sober-faced throughout Abdee's curt announcement, leisurely adding honey to his cup of Peruvian coffee, feeling the softness of the breakfast rolls heaped in a silver wicket basket, finally selecting one dotted with sesame seeds.

Intrigued by the Cuban's lack of curiosity about the nature of this meeting, Abdee stretched back in his chair, confessing, "There is no reason for me to trust you, Soto. In fact, I doubt if I trust you at all. I feel we have too much in common."

Dipping a morsel of the sesame roll into his milky coffee, Soto moved it delicately toward his lips. He still refrained from commenting.

"You came on a rumor to *Castelo Novo Mundo*," Abdee continued. "You know enough about men and the slave trade to have guessed that I planted a rumor in Havana, the story of my returning here with a cargo of valuable slaves. You are probably the only man of the three who recognized my rather cheap ruse."

Still, Soto did not speak.

"You undoubtedly came here to buy. You have gold to spend but your better judgment prevented you from matching Tyler's extravagant bid. And I approve of that."

Soto's greasy lips lifted into a smile. Tucking both hands under his leather belt, Abdee announced, "I would like you, Senor Soto, to sail to Africa for me . . . I have another load of blacks waiting on the Slave Coast."

Slowly raising his head, Soto fixed his beady black eyes on Abdee.

"The *Casa d' Oro* is a sloop," Abdee continued. "A sleeklined, fast-moving vessel which could be fitted to carry five hundred blacks."

Soto resumed chewing his coffee-soaked roll.

"Do you *really* have to return to Havana as quickly as you say?"

Soto shrugged.

Leaning towards him across the corner of the table, Abdee proceeded to explain in detail about his recent agreement with "Store Man," that there would be no less than three hundred Ashanti prisoners on the Slave Coast. Abdee explained that he already possessed the artillery and ammunition which would be traded to the Ibo Tribe for their prisoners.

More slowly now, Abdee explained that if Soto would supply the *Casa d' Oro* to transport the slaves, the price of its rental would be deducted from Abdee's fifty per cent share of the blacks when they were sold in whatever port was offering the highest price for slaves in three month's time.

Furthermore, Abdee added that if slave prices were slack at that future date, they could keep them here at the castle until the prices rose. Abdee said that what in fact he was doing was proposing a temporary partnership between themselves.

Soto's accent was heavy, but his tone as controlled as his mannered actions when he finally spoke. "How do you know, Abdee, that I will not collect these Ashanti slaves and spirit them straight back to my *mercado* in Havana? Why do you believe I would not double-cross you?"

"Because only I can give you the sign by which the African caboceer will know you. He will not sell to another white man."

Soto nodded his head with approval. That was one question settled.

He next asked, "What makes you think that I would not collect the slaves—with this signal—and *then* sail for Cuba?"

Abdee smiled, saying bluntly, "Money."

"Money?"

"An exchange of money."

Soto still did not understand.

"You will give *me* . . . money!"

"I give you money," Soto said, arching one eyebrow, "and you send me on a long voyage across the Atlantic?" He shook his head as if the proposition was insane.

At the moment which Abdee thought that the crafty Cuban was going to reject the offer, Soto's broad chest heaved and he asked, "Can your carpenters build extra shelves in my ship? I sailed from Havana intending to buy no more than two hundred and fifty, three hundred slaves at the most from you. The *Casa d' Oro* is smaller than the *Petit Jour*. It will be a tight pack with any extra slaves."

Abdee readily agreed to the suggestion of carpentry being performed on the *Casa d' Ora* in the castle's workshops, proceeding to discuss the exchange of money, the amount of gold which Ignatio Soto would give him to establish at least a temporary partnership in the Atlantic slave trade with Richard Abdee.

*   *   *

Kinga and Pra, taken from their cells, waited in the Barracoon, standing under guard of two Ibo slaves in the *sale de tormenta* when Abdee finally arrived with a small, white cotton bag in his hand.

Emptying the contents of the bag on a table top, Abdee motioned for Pra to step closer to the table and inspect the necessary equipment. Thin gold wire. Silver needles. Sulphur matches.

Nodding at Kinga, Abdee said to Pra, "That's the woman."

Pra looked quizzically from Abdee, down to the array of shiny equipment, and then back to Kinga.

Realizing that the Ashanti artisan might not understand his words, Abdee motioned for an Ibo guard to bring Kinga closer toward the table.

Ripping off the soiled cloth which wrapped her tall body, Abdee took one of the silver needles between his fingers and mimed the act of piercing for Pra to understand what he wanted. He next pointed at the furry patch between Kinga's legs. Finally, he took a length of thin gold wire and pretended as if he were lacing a hole shut.

Pra smiled. He understood. Abdee's suspicions that Pra would willingly assist him were proving correct.

Pointing down the length of the vaulted dungeon room which had once served as the Portuguese grandee's torture chamber, Abdee drew Pra's attention to a wooden, metal and leather contraption.

He said, "Rack. Kinga will be strapped to that . . . rack." He nodded at Kinga's wrists and ankles.

Pra nodded more fervently. He understood about the rack, too.

"You will not torture her. You will—" he mimed the act of mending a hole, "—*infibulate* her."

Again, Abdee reached toward Kinga's furry patch and, separating the pubic hairs, he took the lips of her vagina between his thumb and forefinger. He motioned Pra to look, too, showing him where he wanted him to pierce the needles. And then, again, Abdee mimed the act of sewing, threading the golden wires through small holes which would be pierced into Kinga's skin. Abdee himself planned to prepare the molten alloy which would adhere the wires and ensure this vaginal infibulation did not come unstuck, that no man would have intercourse with Kinga until he returned to *Castelo Novo Mundo*.

The full phosphorescent circle of the moon lit one side of *Castelo Novo Mundo* that night, causing the fortress to cast a long shadow upon the rippling flatness of the sea. Unlike the dial created by the sun's rays, the dark shadow stretching over the rippling waves in moonlight looked eerie, ominous, a fantasy in a feverish dream.

Few noises emanated from the castellated tower tonight, only the surf kept a metric rhythm around its craggy base, the wind flapping a hemp mat which had not been securely fastened on one of the many inner courts, a plank door creaking from its leather hinges in the breeze. All else was quiet. It was the time to sleep.

But a few people still lay awake in the fortress at this late hour, among them Captain Pennington in his quarters situated at sea level above the Barracoon.

Not listening to the ebbing tide outside his narrow window, Pennington concentrated instead on the black-skinned youth laying astride his back, the ebony male now thrusting his hips against Pennington's upturned buttocks.

The plans which Pennington had made for a Portsmouth cleric to bless his love for Robby had gone awry; Pennington still promised Robby that he would give him his freedom once a man of God somewhere joined them in sacred vows. He hoped to find such a man in New Orleans.

The thought of freedom excited Robby. But he wondered what good freedom would be if he had to live within the confines of Pennington's wifelike jealousy. He could not expose these suspicions to Pennington. He must plot some way to escape the Captain's stifling love. And as Robby drove the oily length of his penis deeper into Pennington's anus, he planned what other prizes he could secure from the doting Englishman—satin breeches, fullsleeve shirts, silver bangles to decorate the sheen of his black skin.

In the yard surrounding the castle's enclosed harbor, the slave girl, Luma, lay on the dirt, her short legs reaching up to her pendulous breasts as she curled in a fetal position around her treasured bullwhip.

Luma had not seen her master mince his first night back from Africa. Still suffering—more mentally than physically—from Abdee's cruel treatment, Luma tried to convince herself tonight that Abdee would not be cruel to her forever. And as she thought about making love to Abdee, she gripped the oily butt of the bullwhip in one fist, slowly easing the butt into the moist hole between her legs, imagining that she was feeling Abdee's manhood deep inside her vagina. She pictured that she and Abdee were making love here in the moonlight, Abdee whispering words of devotion in her ear.

Like Luma, Consuela also entertained thoughts of love tonight but instead of pursuing sexual stimulation, Consuela concentrated on making herself more physically desirable.

Consuela had eaten a full meal tonight but, disappearing quickly into a privy, she stuck her finger down her throat and spewed vomit into a hole which emptied into the sea. She knew this method of losing weight was working, too, because she still had energy to perform her chores and her muslin shift was beginning to bag around her body.

Laying tonight on a pallet in the kitchen, Consuela chewed a mint leaf to sweeten the taste of vomit in her mouth and anxiously prayed her rosary beads. She implored the Holy Madonna to send Claude Saint-Barbot back to *Castelo Novo Mundo*.

Pra's religious inspiration was not Christian. He

sat huddled in a corner of his lone cell tonight in the Barracoon, deliberating the philosphy of African gods, especially the supernatural forces which held men in check by fear and evil curses.

Greegree. Pra felt that a *greegree* was finally working for him, a force stronger than luck which had so far kept him from being killed by Abdee and, now, allowed him at last to gain dominance over Kinga, a woman who ridiculed many of Pra's beliefs.

Pra had felt great spiritual satisfaction inserting the gold wires into Kinga's womanhood earlier today. He smiled to himself now in the blackness of his cell, knowing that his gods would not desert him in the future. Somehow, in some magical and yet unknown way, he would also obtain a chance to seek revenge against the white devil, Richard Abdee, and any black people who remained true to Abdee as followers. The only thing which Pra had to pray for now was his life, and he knew that his *greegree* would spare him, that he would be allowed to escape any death plans which Abdee still might be plotting for him.

Down a damp hallway and around an arched corner from Pra in the Barracoon, Kinga lay on a bed of loose straw in her cell. Her groin burned from the piercing needles and the golden wires now restricting the tender lips of her vagina. The realization of why the wires had been put there was as painful as the bondage itself.

White people were becoming more repulsive to Kinga but she struggled to understand them. She tried to think of their cruel acts in terms of Pra's wickedness.

The Ashanti's name for an evil was *m-fo*. As all Ashantis were not evil like Pra, though, Kinga could not believe that every white man was as wicked as

Richard Abdee. But she believed that only a black person could free her from this perverse bondage.

While Kinga lay awake in the Barracoon, Magnus sprawled across the edge of the bed in Anna Tyler's room. He felt Anna working her mouth on his maleness; he knew that she was kneeling on the floor and watching herself in the cheval mirror.

Anna again had promised Magnus that she would help him some way in the future. And, then, when Abdee had told Magnus this morning that he would need him aboard the *Petit Jour* to transport the slaves to New Orleans, Magnus thought that perhaps his life might indeed soon change. But Anna urged him to be patient, to keep silent about her promise, that she would act at the opportune moment. She had told him those same words again tonight as she prodded at his crotch. And now, as Magnus's penis tingled with stimulation from Anna's mouth, he felt as if his manhood were no longer part of him, that it had no connection to his heart as it wanted to be.

There was only one woman whom Magnus desired. That was Kinga. She was chained to a wall in the Barracoon. How could he help her? He could not even help himself. And thus, Magnus was glad to be sailing tomorrow for New Orleans, hoping that the Tylers would buy him from his master. Anything would be better than staying in *Castelo Novo Mundo*.

Book Two

THE SLAVE PORT

9

THE MISSISSIPPI DELTA

The New Orleans harbor was one of North America's most difficult seaports to enter, its location being in the delta through which the Mississippi River fed into the Gulf of Mexico. Apart from being long and arduous, the approach was complicated by a network of marshy bayous traversed easily only by lighter craft. Expert navigation—and great patience—was required for a large ship to proceed up the Mississippi River to the docks built along the Canal Street harbor.

Politics now added to the complications of sailing the Mississippi Delta. The United States of America had purchased the large tract of land called "The Louisiana Territory." A Napoleonic embargo had only recently been lifted from the port of New Orleans and, as cotton was once again allowed to be exported to England, the waterways, lakes, and bayous were congested with merchant ships.

The *Petit Jour* reached the Mississippi Delta six

days after leaving *Castelo Novo Mundo*, meeting a backup of brigantines, frigates, sloops at the very mouth of the Mississippi River.

Tall masts dotted the purple tint of the late afternoon sky, their rigging crisscrossing one another like spider webbing. Trading ships rode at anchor alongside bulky men-of-war. Freighters stood high in the water, their hulls empty to take on cotton bales for the mills of far off Manchester.

The air was filled with angry shouts, raucous laughter, and blasphemies drifting from the crowded decks. Songs of drunken sailors intermingled with angry curses. The captain of one ship warned another about quartering too closely.

Adding to this congestion of ships, brightly dressed prostitutes had ventured downriver in rented barges from their brothels in New Orleans with hopes of winning business from sailors starved for female companionship.

This knot of sea traffic at the mouth of the Mississippi River was a positive sign that New Orleans was destined to become a major port in the American South, perhaps one of the most vital on the continent. Gold would soon be lining the pocket of planters, brokers, slave dealers, and whores.

* * *

Standing between her husband and Richard Abdee on the forecastle of the *Petit Jour* this late afternoon, Anna Tyler clutched a yellow cashmere shawl under her chin and viewed the jam of sea traffic. She could only occasionally discern a few of the moss-draped oak trees which lined the banks, their roots exposed in the mud and twisting down into the murky water like writhing snakes.

Earlier this year, she had heard about Thomas

Jefferson's negotiation to buy an outsize chunk of the North American continent from Napoleon but she had not expected that the President of the American states would accomplish his ambitious expansions quite this soon.

Considering the changes which "The Louisiana Purchase" represented in terms of money to the Tyler Auction House, Anna slyly smiled as she listened to northern accents mingle with the impatient whines of Creole tradesmen, the singsong voices of black men mixed with the English, Spanish, and French accents. The Babel-like atmosphere surrounding the *Petit Jour* confirmed one thing—she knew for certain now that southern cotton plantations would be crying out for more slaves.

Hugh Tyler viewed the crowd of ships less commercially than his wife, enjoying the visual oddity of sloops cramped against galleons, laughing at the colorful but coarse array of whores as they pushed their barges and pirogues toward the anxious sailors.

Anna scowled at her husband's joviality, cursing him under her breath for being a fool. Couldn't he foresee what four hundred and twenty-five slaves in the hold of this very ship meant for them? The steep prices they could demand? Anna thrilled at the thought of holding an auction sale right here on the mouth of the Mississippi, crying brazenly to the ships around them, announcing to everyone that the *Petit Jour* was laden with African muscle that would ease their labor, slaves to make Louisiana rich!

Checking this impulsive urge, though, Anna glimpsed at Abdee's sombre face. His strong jaw worked impatiently as he also studied the crowd of merchant ships.

Ah, she thought, *that fox does not have a single doubt about the impact which the Louisiana Purchase will have on slave prices. He's probably wishing now he hadn't accepted Hugh's offer quite so readily!*

Ideally, Anna did not want to unload the blacks from the *Petit Jour* immediately upon their arrival at the slip. A wait to inch upriver to a Canal Street mooring could very well give her the precious time she needed to excute a new plan.

Anna saw that somehow she had to go ahead of the *Petit Jour* to New Orleans and find out exactly what was happening in the city. No, she might not wait to sell the slaves in the Tyler Auction House on Duvall Street. If prices were running high for field labor, competitive merchants in other auction houses might pay much larger sums of money than she could ever hope to get on her own auction block. The Tylers' customers were mostly planters, and often those landowners were more judicious in their bidding than a merchant driven insane by the heady phenomenon of supply and demand.

She carefully weighed her advantages. She knew that Richard Abdee had signed an agreement with her husband. Also, Hugh Tyler had agreed to pay ship rental to transport the slaves from the West Indies to Louisiana. She suspected that Abdee badly needed the money. That his capital was tied up in this slave cargo. Also, she knew his love for isolation. He would dread every single minute spent in a bustling city like New Orleans.

Gazing at a thick bank of fog now moving inwards from the gulf, Anna announced in an uneasy tone, "Hugh, I want to try to find a boat to take me upriver. There's no reason for me to wait here in this congestion. I hate it. You can join me or stay aboard. Suit yourself. But I've got to get out of here."

Moving to put his arm around her, he said, "Now don't go getting fidgety, honey. We'll move on soon."

Slipping free of his grasp, she wondered how she had ever married such a stupid man? Any clever person would immediately suspect her motive for leaving. She only hoped that Abdee did not find her sudden departure suspicious.

"Hugh," she continued more firmly, "don't press me to stay cooped up here for a moment longer. I want to go . . . home!"

"It won't be long, honey. I'll find a patrol boat. They'll tell us exactly how long we have to wait."

Moving still farther away from him, she said, "It's sweet of you, Hugh, to try and coax me to stay with you. But please let me go on alone. The time will give you an opportunity to persuade Mister Abdee to—" she decided that the time had come to say it,"—sell us Magnus."

Hugh jerked his head, surprised at her announcement. True, he had mentioned to her than he would be interested in buying Magnus. But he had understood that she did not approve of the idea. Apart from having already spent so much money on Abdee slaves, Hugh remembered Anna complaining about educated blacks. Evidently, she had changed her mind.

"Yes, I thought about what you told me and you're absolutely right, Hugh. We could use a man like that. The Lord only knows you don't spend enough time on Duvall Street."

Lowering his voice, he said, "Honey, we haven't even discussed a price."

"Offer Mister Abdee five thousand dollars for Magnus and see what he says."

"Five thousand dollars!" Hugh stared at her in amazement. It was an outlandish offer.

Abdee had been standing near to the Tylers, watching them, listening to their exchange. He did not know what she was trying to achieve by deserting the ship before they reached harbor. One thing he knew for certain, though, was that he was not going to let her maneuver him like she did her husband.

He called, "You forget, I do not sell my people, Mrs. Tyler."

"Not even for a very good price? I would be willing to pay five thousand dollars for a nigger who can keep ledgers in an auction house."

The mention of five thousand dollars made Abdee pause. He immediately saw himself putting it toward the price of a plantation. He also thought about returning to *Castelo Novo Mundo* with Magnus and realized that Kinga might well prefer a personable black man rather than himself. Such an incident could cause many problems. But, still, he hated seeing Anna Tyler having her way.

Abdee abruptly turned toward Magnus sitting with a group of sailors around a stanchion. He beckoned him to join them.

As Magnus smiled across the deck, Abdee announced, "The Tylers have just offered me five thousand dollars for you, Magnus. Mrs. Tyler claims that she has plans for you to hold a position in her slave house."

Anna gave him a quick nod, assuring Magnus that what Abdee said was true.

Abdee looked more closely at Magnus, his mind quickly weighing the importance of five thousand dollars. He realized that, when he did move to a plantation, he would need a proper overseer. Magnus's dangerous attraction to Kinga outweighed his future usefulness. Abdee asked, "What do you think, Magnus? Would you like to stay in New Orleans?"

Magnus began to speak but, stopping, he slowly shook his head. He had only dreamt about hearing such a question. It was the only way to forget about Kinga.

Hugh Tyler interrupted, "Abdee, I find it ungentlemanly of you to be discussing this matter with the nigger himself."

"No," Anna said boldly, let the liberal . . . Master Abdee have his way. Let him allow Magnus to make his own choice. This could be interesting to hear, Hugh."

Turning to Magnus, she asked, "Do you want to come with us, Magnus? If you do, the papers can be drawn up immediately. Captain Pennington can witness the sale as an uninvolved party." She only hoped that Magnus remembered the promises she had made to him during their lovemaking at *Castelo Novo Mundo*. She had not suspected that she would ever have to honor her promises, but neither had she envisaged that she could use Magnus against that bastard, Richard Abdee.

Confused and too anxious to speak his mind, Magnus dipped his broad shoulders, grinning like a boy, rubbing his shaven head, looking down at his canvas shoes.

Anna pushed, "Can we take your silence as a 'Yes' . . . Magnus?"

Her annoying insistence decided the matter for Abdee. He said, "Mrs. Tyler. You still do not understand. I do not sell my people. If Magnus wants to go with you, he leaves me a free man. Manumission papers can be prepared as quickly as a deed of sale. I'll have Pennington do it right now."

Anna reeled at Abdee's announcement. She thought, *The bastard. He's called my bluff. What am I going to do with a free nigger?*

Abdee enjoyed the shocked expressions on both Anna's and Hugh Tyler's faces. They couldn't believe his sudden generosity. The gesture of freeing Magnus was worth losing five thousand dollars. Abdee doubted if he would have done the same thing ten, even five years ago. But ten, even five years ago, he was a younger man. Abdee's friendship with black slaves like Magnus had taught him one important fact—despite the fact that many people considered Negroes to be animals, many women often preferred a black man to a white one. Especially if the buck was young and handsome like Magnus. And this fact was doubly true if the woman were black herself . . . like Kinga. No, Abdee realized that he did not need trouble like that. Magnus must leave.

*   *   *

Hugh Tyler had decided to leave the *Petit Jour* with Anna when Captain Pennington had drawn up Magnus's manumission papers. Finding a barge to carry them upriver, the Tylers took Magnus with them and promised Abdee that they would collect the slaves from the *Petit Jour* and pay him in full when the ship finally docked at the Canal Street harbor.

Although tired from the sea voyage, Hugh Tyler knew that if he stayed home tonight Anna would not allow him to rest. He would have to stay up listening to her talk about business, explaining the ways in which she planned to learn how the Louisiana Purchase had affected the price of slave labor in their absence. Also, she would undoubtedly make a few barbed remarks about his incompetence as an administrator, saying how glad she was to have some one— even if he were black—to help her tackle the many chores at the auction house. Anna had told Hugh that it would be easier to house Magnus for the moment in the servants' quarters at their home.

Not having the energy nor the patience to argue

with Anna tonight, Hugh decided to join a Creole friend, Maurice Billaud, for a drink. The two men then went to visit the latest bordello which had opened in New Orleans. Billaud promised that the establishment offered the best show in town.

Settling back into a red plush chair placed on the edge of a small stage swagged with scarlet velvet, Hugh Tyler lit a cheroot cigar and told himself to forget about Anna and her obsession to discuss slave prices. He told himself to relax, to enjoy the show at this new pleasure house.

Many bordellos in New Orleans staged fantasies but Billaud had promised that the one here was extraordinary. The madame of the brothel was a free black woman from the island of St. Kitts. Billaud also explained now that, because the Negress's skin was supposedly marred by burns, no one ever saw her face. She constantly kept her head heavily veiled. According to Billaud, the proprietress's name was Naomi but the noise in the small stage room was too loud for Hugh to hear the name of the bordello. He was too tired, too disinterested to ask him to repeat it. It did not matter.

Spotting Negresses dressed in scanty corsets beginning to snuff the candles in the surrounding chandeliers with long phallic shaped cups on the end of brass poles, Hugh concentrated on the stage in the center of the smoke-filled room.

First, three young Negro men wandered across the red moquette. They wore carved wooden and brightly painted African masks on their heads, the rest of their athletic bodies completely bare. As a drum began to beat slowly in the background, Hugh Tyler guessed that the men were supposed to be on the African continent.

This hunch proved to be correct when a white

woman appeared, dragging a long fish net in one hand and a whip in the other. She wore thigh-high black leather boots, a red jewelled bolero, and a scanty red patch covering her pubic hairs—nothing else except for a red tricorne hat atop her mound of yellow curls.

The fact that this statuesque female represented a slave dealer was made even clearer when she began to crack her whip at the three black men in tribal masks. Then, tossing the fish net over their heads, she pulled them toward her in a heap.

Falling among them as the sound of the offstage drums grew louder, the woman's pale body became entangled in an orgy of muscular brown legs and arms, and the width of fish netting.

The three Africans squirmed and writhed in a stylized manner. And after ridding themselves of the masks and throwing aside the netting, they began to subjugate the woman . . . to the audience's delight!

Two of the muscular men held the blond woman by the arms and forced her to lay across the knee of the third Negro. He began to slap at her pale buttocks, spanking her naked flesh slowly at first, first smiting one cheek, then the next, slapping one side of her buttocks with the top of his hand, the other side with the hand's flatness.

The rhythm gaining momentum, the sound of spanking grew louder and the woman's buttocks began to turn a bright shade of pink. Suddenly, one of the men let go of her arm and stood in front of her face.

Then, while she was being spanked now in a severe manner, the black man stood in front of her, making her take his firm phallus in her mouth.

The blond "slaver" worked voraciously on him

and, when the spanking soon subsided, she squirmed her glowing pink cheeks to take the phallus of the man who had been punishing her.

Soon, the woman lay on the stage floor, still greedily mouthing one penis, squirming to take the second penis in her anus as that man lay behind her. And, now, the third man lay down on the moquette in front of her, ripping off the red sequined patch from between her legs and beginning to drive himself into her vagina.

The audience cheered and applauded as the blond "slaver" greedily worked, pumped, and gyrated to accommodate all three over-sized phalluses.

The virile "Africans" suddenly began to groan as the woman maintained her voracious appetite by flexing, contracting, working all three orifices. She continued to gratify each of them in separate ways until, slowly, the Negroes were no longer dominating her. The blond woman was draining life from them. They were slowly succumbing to her sexual prowess.

First, one man reached his explosion. Then, the next, and the third. And, as they fell back onto the mosquette limp, defeated, spent, the blond woman jumped quickly to her feet and stood triumphantly over their tawny, perspiration-covered bodies clustered in a glistening heap.

Despite the wild applause and laughter filling the bordello's small theatre, Hugh Tyler remained seated soberly in his chair. He was thinking again of his wife.

Having watched this tableau of a white woman voraciously satisfying herself with black men, his mind kept going back to Anna. He thought that there might be a slight possibility that Anna had so readily agreed to buy Magnus for some reason other than for him to work in their auction house. Perhaps Anna did not hate black men as much as she pretended. That she and this stage "slave dealer" had much in common.

Hugh Tyler knew that his wife was definitely keeping some personal fact from him. And the more that he thought about the matter, the more convinced he felt that she might be trying to dupe him.

He decided to make an arrangement with Anna's maid. He would bribe the black girl, Lillibette, to spy on her mistress. Hugh Tyler knew that he could buy Lillibette's cooperation with one gold eagle, a cheap price to pay to learn if he was as dumb as Anna had always claimed. Yes, he would talk to Lillibette this very night.

10
LYNN & CRADDOCK, AUCTIONEERS

New Orleans had undergone many changes in the six years since Abdee had last been here, but his mind was too occupied with other matters the next day when he hailed a carriage to notice how the bayou town had transformed into one of the most vital cities in the American South.

Streets in New Orleans which not long ago had been no more than dirt tracks were now cobbled and drains had been built alongside them to accommodate the tropical rainfall. Buildings rose higher than the former one room shanties. Tradesmen now prospered inside elegantly furnished emporiums. But the cries of hawkers still remained a part of New Orleans street life, Negresses singsonging that they had cray fish for sale, Creole crones hissing to passersby that they could read the future in a deck of Tarot cards, half-naked picaninnies selling oysters on the half shell, flower and herb vendors pushing wooden carts festooned with garlands of their dried or fresh wares.

Riding from the Canal Street wharf in the hired conveyance, Abdee slouched back on the cracked brown leather seat, staring blankly at the smudged glows of the gas streetlights which enshrouded most of the street activity. The fog had grown thicker in the last twenty-four hours, now totally blanketing this district of New Orleans called *Vieux Carre*, only adding to Abdee's oppressive mood.

After finally having secured an anchor at the Canal Street harbor late last night, Abdee began to regret that he had agreed to transport the slaves from *Castelo Novo Mundo* to New Orleans. He felt that this voyage was somehow going to evolve into a nightmare for him.

The first problem had begun yesterday, after he had decided to grant Magnus his manumission. Captain Pennington had retired to his cabin to write the necessary documents, grudgingly allowing Samuel Tewes to con the *Petit Jour* upriver.

Pennington's cabin boy, Robby, had disappeared sometime during the period in which Pennington had gone to his cabin and the time that the Tylers, along with Magnus, had departed from the *Petit Jour* in a rented barge.

Searching the ship from stern to prow, Pennington even descended into the stench of the slave hull in the quest for his precious Robby, an area of the ship he never visited. But he could find Robby nowhere.

This morning, Pennington had hysterically accused Abdee of allowing the boy to escape when he had been forced to compose Magnus's manumission papers. That the boy had jumped down into one of the small boats moving up through the crowd of ships.

In a heat of temper, Abdee crudely insinuated

that, if Robby had been missing from Pennington's bed last night, the reason must be that the boy had grown weary of satisfying an old man's perverse lust. That Robby had scrambled ashore for more natural— and younger— pickings!

The rash words had struck closer to the truth of the matter than Abdee had intended. Pennington had blustered, tightening his fists until his knuckles turned white. He had not spoken again to Abdee this morning aboard ship, except to mumble some gibberish about the Lord seeking his own revenge on the wicked.

Riding along the fogbound streets, Abdee now listened to the hollow sound which the horses's hooves made against the cobblestones and brooded about a problem which troubled him more than Pennington's petulant moods.

By this morning, the Tylers still had not come, nor sent an agent, to collect the four hundred and twenty-five slaves from the *Petit Jour* at the Canal Street harbor and pay him for the slaves.

Abdee decided that the Tylers had tried his patience enough. They had pushed him too far. Still seething about the way in which Anna Tyler had offered to buy Magnus, Abdee had no doubt that she had purposely been out to annoy him yesterday. That she was now purposely postponing the collection of the slaves.

As the black coachman now reined the team of dappled horses in front of a tall, white building on Rampart Street, he shouted, "Lynn and Craddock, Sir!"

Abdee looked soberly at the building, his eyes focusing on a brass plaque embedded to the right side of the tall wrought iron gate—MESSRS. LYNN AND CRADDOCK, AUCTION HOUSE.

Quickly reviewing his scheme of ignoring his written agreement with Hugh Tyler, Abdee decided that, yes, he would try to sell the four hundred and twenty-five slaves to another auction house. He tossed a few coins toward the driver and, resettling the low-crowned hat squarely over his weatherworn face, Abdee stubbornly marched up the front steps of the auctioneers to introduce himself to its owners. He knew that he must act quickly to avoid trouble.

* * *

Hiram Craddock was a frail, stoop-shouldered man, somewhere around sixty years, Abdee guessed. He first saw him hunched over a marbleized ledger in his sparsely furnished office on the second floor of the Rampart Street auction house.

When Abdee began to tell Craddock about the cargo of slaves anchored on Canal Street, though, Craddock excitedly unsnapped his sleeve guards, replaced his green visor with a wide-brimmed straw hat, and moved with the agility of a much younger man as he hurried to investigate what he called "priceless black ivory."

Craddock insisted on driving Abdee to Canal Street in his open buggy. As he snapped the whip over the head of his chestnut mare, he leaned one ear toward Abdee to listen for more details about the slaves, anxiously nodding when Abdee explained that the Africans came mostly from the Ashanti, Kru and Mundingo tribes.

Samuel Tewes met the buggy at the wharf, taking Abdee aside to report that, first, Captain Pennington had gone ashore to search for his cabin boy, and, secondly, the Tylers had still not come to collect the slaves. Tewes answered with a knowing wink when Abdee told him to keep the Tylers off the *Petit Jour* if they came while Hiram Craddock was still down in the hold.

Escorting Craddock across the deck, Abdee proceeded him down the ladder and, with a bulls-eye lantern, he stood alongside the merchant as he began to make an exploratory investigation.

Craddock progressed from shelf to shelf, inspecting each Negro with the expertise of a man who knew what would or would not sell to his regular customers. He studied feet, hands, mouths, asking for certain bucks to be unchained. He peered in their mouths, pulled back foreskins, told them to grip their ankles. Craddock's grunts of approval assured Abdee that he was pleased with what he found.

Finished with this quick but thorough examination, Craddock followed Abdee up the ladder and, brushing at his sharkskin jacket, he said, "Sir, you place me in somewhat of a dilemma . . ."

Abdee waited.

"It is no secret that we are badly in need of slaves to sell. You have a prime load here. Indeed you do. I will not even try to bargain with you for low prices. I would gladly offer you top scale prices but . . ."

Shaking his head, Craddock continued more glumly, "We quite frankly do not have the money to pay for your kind of blacks. The markets have been slow up to now. We have no cash reserves."

Abdee could think of nothing except to leave New Orleans as quickly as possible. He said brashly, "Make me an offer."

"I could only make an offer that would insult you, Mister Abdee. You would never contact me in the future. I do not want to risk that. Not after seeing the grade of blacks you sell."

"What about raising money from a bank?"

"That's what I'm thinking. But banks dawdle and

hold long-winded meetings. You told me in my office that you had to sell quickly. You might have to wait until next week if I went to a bank." He shrugged helplessly.

Abdee would rather take the slaves back to *Castelo Novo Mundo* than to stay in New Orleans for a full week. He began to shake his head.

"Can you let me have at least until tomorrow?" Hiram Craddock asked. "Give me time to talk to my partner, Benson Lynn."

Abdee said, "I will have to have your answer the first thing tomorrow morning. No later." He added after quick consideration, "There are of course other houses interested but, for personal reasons, I would rather not do business with them."

Craddock nodded his head, indicating that he understood. And rather than pursuing the point of competitors, he assured Abdee, "I will do everything in my power to oblige us both. And as quickly as possible."

And, thus, it was arranged for Richard Abdee to meet Hiram Craddock tomorrow morning for his answer. It was then, when Abdee accompanied Craddock down the gangplank to the dock that the auctioneer looked at the name of the ship scrawled on the prow's peeling paint. He said, "The *Petit Jour!* That name means 'twilight' in French, doesn't it?"

Abdee nodded. Having felt a curious rapport with Craddock up to now, he did not want the man to ruin it by becoming inquisitive.

Craddock mused, "It's not often a man sees a name like that. It's even stranger considering the only other 'Petit Jour' I know."

"What place is that?" Abdee asked, wondering if Craddock had known the estate, *Petit Jour*, on St. Kitts which he had renamed to Dragonard Plantation.

His eyes twinkling, Craddock teased, "I don't know if I should tell you this, Mister Abdee, not wanting to offend a prospective colleague."

"You'll learn I'm not easily offended, Mister Craddock."

Smiling, Craddock explained, "A new fancy house has opened here in New Orleans. It's called that, too, *Petit Jour*."

"A fancy house? You mean a brothel?"

"Exactly. A splendid new brothel on Rampart Street."

Smiling, Abdee confided, "I was thinking of going to such a place myself. Perhaps I should pay a visit on this other . . . *Petit Jour*."

Stopping then, he shook his head, saying, "No, I think not. I've spent enough time on my *Petit Jour*. I don't need another. Not tonight."

Craddock promptly supplied the name of another bordello, offering to drive Abdee to The Esplanade himself, explaining that it was the most frequented house in New Orleans still despite the *Petit Jour* slowly gaining in popularity.

11

A DEMANDING MASTER

Richard Abdee had not been to a bordello since living on St. Kitts. He had stopped his visits there when he had moved the Negress, Naomi, to Dragonard Plantation and she became his mistress. Naomi had been the madam of Basseterre's most notorious brothel, Chez Naomi, on Barracks Lane.

Tonight's Negress was a statuesque octoroon called Ella. Or was it Stella? Or Mariella? Abdee could not remember. Nor did he care. He had consumed more than a bottle of black rum and wanted a paid woman to please him, his sexual appetite having been made more keen by the confusion in his life. A desire for total domination over a female surged inside his veins.

Ella—Stella, or Mariella—entered the garishly furnished bedroom in the bordello, The Esplanade, this early evening in a self-assured manner. She wore red satin pumps, a cream negligee which hung half-tied around her naked body, exposing the *cafe au lait* brownness of her breasts. Towering on the pair of red satin pumps, she surveyed Abdee's naked body sprawled back on the brass bed.

Brazenly, she inquired about his sexual preferences as she picked at the fingercurls lining her forehead. She sank down onto the edge of the feather mattress before Abdee had time to speak and reached toward the softness of his masculinity, weighing it in the palm of her hand as if she were inspecting a sausage in a shop.

Abdee's masculinity immediately responded to the touch of the prostitute's hand. But ignoring her clucks of approval, and aggravated by her superior air, he reached forward and, grabbing her thin wrists, pulled the woman toward him.

Nostrils flaring, the octoroon prostitute resisted the pressure of his grasp. She struggled against him, warning, "If you like it rough, Jacko, let me make one thing clear to you . . ."

Before the woman had time to finish, Abdee strengthened his grasp and flung her onto the mattress. Then, quickly moving to sit astride her shoulders, he jammed his crotch toward her startled face and said as he glared down at her, "I don't want to hear you ever mention how I like it, bitch! I just want to . . . do it."

His masculinity was hardening as his authority over the woman increased. He felt her half-naked body tighten beneath him with terror. He watched his penis lengthen above her face with excitement.

Cautious that she might sink her sharp white teeth into his phallus, Abdee avoided her mouth, instead poking the throbbing erection at her cheeks, her throat, her eyes. He kept his voice at a monotone, talking to her in language which was at first abusive and, then, slowly he began to explain the subservient role he expected her to play to his male dominance. He reminded the octoroon prostitute that she was not dealing with some backwoods planter, that she was not going to fake a few groans and collect her money. He told her that he didn't think that she was worthy enough for him to copulate with, that she would be fortunate if he even allowed her to fetch his boots from across the room, that he might only let her rub his boots against the stinking hole between her legs.

Slowly easing his hold around her wrists, Abdee jerked open her negligee and moved one hand down her breasts, tightening his thumb and forefinger over her now taut nipples, his other hand kneading the warmth between her legs.

Her body was still tense. He recognized, though, that the rigidness no longer came from terror. She was sexually excited now. She was responding to Abdee's power over her.

The octoroon prostitute no longer spoke of making facts clear to Abdee. She obediently dropped her negligee to the floor. She forgot about time, about activities outside this red-flocked room. She let herself be led into a hypnotic course of actions, hungrily applying kisses to his penis, holding his testicles in her mouth, running her lips down the hairs which coated his legs, his thighs, his calves brushing more adoring kisses against his feet.

On the floor, the prostitute crouched like an adoring slave, rising to rub her furry patch against his shins, murmuring for Abdee's permission to hold his manhood in her mouth, reaching her arms adoringly up to his shoulders towering above her, begging that, although she knew she was not good enough for him, would he make love to her?

Crack! Abdee slapped her across the face. Before she had time to whine, to cry for mercy, he placed both hands beneath her arms and flung her naked back onto the bed. And roughly spreading her legs, he stood next to the bed and leaned forward to pierce the wetness now glistening between her legs.

Begging at first for him to stop, complaining that he had mistreated her enough, the prostitute tossed her head from side to side on the mattress, squirming to escape his slaps, jabs, taunts.

But Abdee's grip on her legs was too firm to escape; his phallus was excited by this dominance and he drove deeper between her vaginal lips. The woman's agonized pleading fed his appetite for power. He stared dull-eyed down at himself slicking in and out of her black public hairs, slowly smiling as he saw her beginning to contract and expand for him.

When the woman's words slowly turned to praise again, Abdee muttered for her to shut her mouth. He called her a slut, commanding her to grip both breasts, to pinch her nipples, to push her midsection toward him, to twist sideways, to raise one leg higher to add variation for his enjoyment.

The sight of this abject obedience to him, heightened by the finesse of this prostitute's skills, and Abdee felt himself cresting to an explosion as he drilled deeper and deeper inside her.

Also, the thought of another person behaving with such servility to him, excited Abdee as much as the visual thrill. Thinking of his need to command, to succeed, to be a master, his entire body seemed to surge with power. He felt an explosion again, an eruption which engulfed his entire body. He drove harder, deeper, rougher, working to unleash the last drop of his hunger . . .

Abdee was not aware of the prostitute again until

he tossed sleepily on the feather mattress. He felt her lips gently brushing his naked body. Her fingers eagerly worked to arouse his masculinity again. She whispered praise as if participating in some pagan worship.

Drowsily remembering that he was in a New Orleans bordello called The Esplanade, he next recalled a prostitute named Ella . . . or was it Stella? Rolling on his side, Abdee muttered for the woman to leave the room. He wanted to catch a bit more sleep in a decent bed before he returned to his quarters aboard the *Petit Jour*. He had no further use for the woman. Tomorrow night, he decided, he might try that other place, *Petit Jour*.

* * *

Robby smiled knowingly at the man with the mouth full of silver teeth. He had never seen silver teeth before. He had seen many things last night and all today in the harbor district of New Orleans which he had never seen before. He had seen snaggled-toothed crones selling sprigs of violets. He had seen brightly dressed Negresses carrying baskets full of melons and fruit atop their heads. He had seen small children with armsful of seashell necklaces. Robby had wanted one of the seashell necklaces very badly but, when the children discovered that he had no money, they turned their backs on him, continuing down the narrow streets and shouting for other people to buy their wares. They left Robby depressed and sad because he had no money but, as he wandered deeper into *Vieux Carre*, his eyes widened at the elaborate wrought iron verandas and balconies on the colorfully painted buildings. He gawked at the velvet and satin clothes on the most beautiful women he had ever seen. He watched them twirl their parasols as they stopped to visit with one another on the boardwalks. He followed men dressed in stylishly cut clothes until they told him to leave them alone. Robby again felt that everyone hated him, that he might be better off by returning to the ship and resume his dreary life as the fat English captain's boyfriend, but then suddenly he saw the man with silver teeth smiling at him from a deep doorway. The man was not handsome nor dressed in stylish clothes, but neither was he as fat as Captain Pennington. Robby hoped that he would not be so possessive and jealous as Captain Pennington. He hoped that this man would not read and read and read to him from the Bible and then preach boring sermons on how the Lord had predestined them to meet and become married. *Married?* Robby laughed. Here he was thinking that the man might be willing to take care of him and buy him presents, when all that the stranger had done so far was flash his mouthful of precious teeth. Seeing the stranger begin to work his hand inside one pocket of his trousers, Robby felt his throat turn dry. The stranger was interested in him! He was making a secret signal! And as Robby stepped closer, working his own hand over the bulge inside his ragged osnaburgh breeches, he smiled back to the man, showing that he was willing to go with him. Robby was thinking how much money a man with silver teeth must have, imagining all the beautiful things that he could buy for him, when he suddenly felt someone grab him around the neck. A handkerchief was pressed over his nose and mouth and he saw the smile disappear on the stranger's face as he quickly instructed the man behind Robby, "Hold the nigger pansy-boy until the drug takes hold. Then shove him into the cart with the rest." That was all that Robby remembered hearing.

12

THE MERCHANT'S STORY

The fog began to lift the next morning, the winds already shifting it southwards to the gulf when Abdee returned to the *Petit Jour* from The Esplanade. He was in a strange mixture of fatigue and anxiety. He did not even feel sexually satisfied by his encounter with the prostitute. He collapsed fully-clothed onto his bed, drifting into a half-sleep and, thinking how he would like a repeat sexual bout with some woman—any woman—Abdee's phallus hardened.

The thud of footsteps on deck awakened him from an unsatisfactory sleep. His waking thoughts were again about the Tylers. They had finally come to collect the slaves!

Jumping from the bed, Abdee lucidly decided that he would send the Tylers away. He would tell them that their agreement was cancelled. That they could not treat him so off-handedly. He then heard a pounding on the door of his cabin.

Swinging open the door, prepared to attack whomever he saw on the otherside, Abdee was surprised to see Hiram Craddock standing there. A broad grin crossed the wiry old man's face as he announced, "Mister Abdee, I have good news for you."

Abdee waited, thinking that it was about time that he heard some good news.

Craddock explained, "I went to the bank after our meeting yesterday. They have given me the money to buy the slaves at what I think is a reasonable price for both of us."

Abdee broke into a grin. Hell, he thought, I haven't smiled since . . . how long? Years?

Craddock continued, "To arrive at a fair price, I had to do a little homework. I snooped around New Orleans a bit and found out how much a load like this would normally fetch. Let's say, I'll offer forty-five thousand dollars for the slaves. And to cover the cost of their transport here . . . an extra five thousand? That shouldn't put you at too much of a loss?"

He knew! Craddock knew he was matching Tyler's offer to the last cent. He had somehow found out about Abdee's contract with the Tylers!

Raising his finger, Craddock playfully shamed, "That was a very unethical thing to do, Mister Abdee, agreeing to sell to one auction house and then going to their competitors. Very unethical indeed. But then there are many people who say our trade is not based on ethics. And some say that the Tyler Auction House— just to pick a name out of the blue, you understand—is the least ethical of all us devils!"

Shaking his head in amazement, Abdee said, "I don't know why we haven't done business before, Mister Craddock. But one thing I do know, we will certainly do business in the future." He was thinking specifically about the cargo of Ashantis which Ignatio

Soto would soon be delivering from the Slave Coast.

Craddock assured him, "Oh, but we have done business before, Mister Abdee. That is, if you're the same Richard Abdee who owned the Dragonard Plantation on St. Kitts."

Abdee slowly nodded, but sobering now at the mention of his past. Waving his hand at Abdee, Craddock said casually, "Let me tell you about that after I give orders to my men. I would like to start unloading the Africans right away. A large consignment of tobacco is scheduled into this dock at midday. I would like to have the coffles moved out of here by then."

Abdee readily agreed to Hiram Craddock bringing his roustabouts immediately aboard the *Petit Jour*, letting them unload the slaves from the hold. He told the merchant that he would rouse the cook to make a pot of strong black coffee which they could share when Craddock returned to tell his story—and pay Abdee the money in cash.

* * *

Abdee had not heard the name Ta-Ta in years.

Sitting across the cabin table from Craddock in the warm afternoon sunlight pouring through his mullioned window, Abdee listened attentively as the merchant recounted how his firm, Lynn and Craddock, had sold three slaves from Dragonard Plantation in St. Kitts seven years ago to an upcountry Louisiana Plantation called The Star. Craddock recalled selling a Negro wench, Ta-Ta, and two half-caste children, one child named Monk and a dusky-skinned infant named Pierre.

Pierre? Abdee clearly remembered Ta-Ta, his French wife's personal maid at Dragonard Plantation. Monkey was the son whom he himself had sired with

Ta-Ta. But Abdee could not imagine who the other child might be—Pierre.

Although the incident had happened well over five years ago now, Abdee definitely remembered that Ta-Ta and Monkey had left St. Kitts with his wife, Honore. The three of them had fled the plantation in a pony cart, going to Basseterre to escape Abdee in a convoy of ships sailing for France. He remembered, too, that Honore had been pregnant at the time. He now wondered if Pierre might be . . . no, the idea was absurd.

Listening more closely to Craddock's story, Abdee learned that Ta-Ta, Monkey and Pierre had been brought to New Orleans by a woman evangelist who had purchased them cheaply from buccaneers in East Florida.

Pierre? Abdee remembered that Honore's brother had also been called Pierre.

Pierre Jubrot had challenged him to a duel on St. Kitts, Abdee killing him at the boundary of three northern parishes. Recalling the strange relationship which Honore had had with her perverse brother, Abdee also remembered how very fond she had been of him. Yes, perhaps she might have given Pierre's name to her son.

Despite the recollections of these facts which he had tried to keep blocked from his memory, Abdee still could not accept the fact that he had a son someplace in Louisiana. That his own flesh and blood had been sold into slavery! A child born of a black woman—like Monkey born of Ta-Ta—had Negro blood in its veins. That was a different matter. Monkey was a slave. He should be rightfully kept in bondage. But a child born of his French wife . . . a son of his . . . no, it could never happen.

Abdee looked stonily ahead as Craddock repeated what little the auction house had been told concerning the background of Ta-Ta and the two half-caste boys. The wench had been touted as having the ability to speak French fluently and possessing the qualifications for acting as a lady's maid. According to Craddock's information, Ta-Ta's former mistress had died of consumption in East Florida when the French ship on which she had been sailing back diverted from its course because of flareups in the then increasing political revolts in France.

Honore, dead? Abdee had not thought of Honore in years and the possibility now that she might have suffered a miserable death did not move him. He had never loved Honore. He had only married her to gain control of *Petit Jour*, the plantation on St. Kitts which he had developed, enlarged and renamed Dragonard Plantation.

Up to this moment, Abdee had always believed that his wife had returned to France. The few times that he thought about the matter, he took for granted that she had probably given birth to the child there. He had never thought about himself planting a life seed in Honore's womb. The rare times that he had bedded her, he had done so for some ulterior reason of his own. How could he then become vexed later about the possibility of an offspring? Neither had Abdee ever concerned himself about the gender of an offspring, whether he had become a father of a son or daughter. As Honore had been a physically weak woman anyway, Abdee had even predicted that she would probably give birth to a stillborn child, or one with physical deformities. Neither thought had ever troubled him.

But . . . a slave?

Craddock's voice now seemed to Abdee to be coming from the far end of a tunnel, listening as the merchant explained how the Star Plantation was only a day's hard ride to the north of New Orleans. And as he knew that its master, Albert Selby, rarely sold his slaves, Craddock suspected that Ta-Ta and the two half-caste children were probably still bonded to The Star.

This announcement sobered Abdee, destroyed the good mood he had been enjoying no more than half an hour ago when Craddock had agreed to buy his slave cargo. He told himself that he did not need to be troubled with catastrophes in other people's lives. Hadn't he always been his own master? Hadn't his goals always been to establish a total independence for himself in the world? He had turned his back many years ago on his own family in England, even selling his peerage for a warehouse of rum in Basseterre. So what right did fortune have now to face him with the fact that he, a man struggling to be indominable, had a son somewhere in the world living as . . . a slave?

* * *

"Robby?"

It was almost noon now and Thomas Pennington had not been back to the *Petit Jour* all night, searching the harbor streets and winding alley ways of *Vieux Carre* for his cabin boy, promising himself that if he found him—*when* he found him—that he would quit his captainship and then settle down here with Robby in New Orleans.

Between asking passersby if they had seen a boy fitting the description of Robby, and asking in shops or cafes if a Negro youth had come requesting food or shelter, Pennington became more desperate over the disappearance of his loved one.

At first blaming himself for not keeping a watchful eye on Robby, Pennington next saw Abdee as being responsible. Abdee! If Abdee had not sent him to make out the manumission papers for Magnus, Robby might not have slipped off the ship.

Visualizing how the boy could have easily crowded into one of the many pirogues which had moved through the congestion of ships crowding for the harbor that night, Pennington smiled at the boy's pluck but also cried over losing him.

"Robby?"

Pennington did not know how long he could search. He tried not to think of what he would do if he didn't find him. The thought of sailing back to *Castelo Novo Mundo* without Robby made his stomach ache. He cursed *Castelo Novo Mundo*. He cursed slavery. He cursed Abdee's greed for money which had brought them to New Orleans.

Standing now on the corner of two intersecting streets, he raised both hands to his mouth to shout again, oblivious of the passersby who stared at him calling so remorsefully.

At that moment he heard a wagon rattle from a courtyard, the driver lashing the horses while a man sitting next to the driver on the wooden seat shook his fist at Pennington, calling him a blind fool.

Catching his breath at coming so close to being trampled by horses, Pennington stared as the wagon thundered up the street, a canvas securely tied over its deep bed, the angry man still shaking his fist in fury, still shouting obscenities and baring a mouthful of silver teeth. Pennington felt a chill pass over him. He decided then to return to the ship, to have a badly needed nap and resume his search later tonight. He knew how much Robby loved to lurk around at night.

13

OAKBANKS

Life inside the Tylers' columned house named "Oak-banks" confused Magnus. Located in the district of New Orleans called Bayou St. John, "Oakbanks" sat within a sprawling park surrounded by moss-draped oak trees, the house and stables having the cool elegance of many plantation manors located further up the Mississippi River, places which Magnus had seen as a child when his master had taken him on trips south from Natchez.

Hugh Tyler had not come back to Oakbanks from the family business establishment on Duvall Street again tonight. the second night since the *Petit Jour* had reached New Orleans. Anna Tyler had spent most of the day—and yesterday—at the auction house, returning home in vile moods.

After eating supper alone in the dining room, she waited until the house slaves retired to their quarters before she crept down the steps to where Magnus was assigned to a room in the cellar and beckoned him to follow her up the backstairs to her bedroom.

Although Magnus did not see himself being happy in the future as a "fancy," a black man kept in a fine house merely for the sexual pleasure of a white master or mistress, he believed that being a fancy was what Anna Tyler intended for him. He did not know what arrangement she would make with her jealous husband about keeping a stud in their house but he felt wary of the present situation.

There had been no further mention of Magnus working as a freeman in the Tyler Auction House; in fact, he had seen little change in his life since receiving manumission. The only difference now was that Anna had stopped calling him "boy" or "slave." And he suspected that that was only temporary.

The idleness in the last forty-eight hours, and the uncertainty about his future, kindled Magnus's sexual desires. But Anna's sexual appetite had temporarily disappeared. She avoided his groping hands again tonight, motioning him to go lay on her bed while she paced her bedroom and talked to him. She was using Magnus more and more as a confidant.

❖   ❖   ❖

Picking up a blue-and-white Chinese vase, Anna hurled it across the bedroom, the crash bringing Magnus's wandering mind back to the bedroom. He stared at the chips of the china vase lying on the carpet and called to Anna, "Why you do that?"

Not answering, Anna jerked in frustration at the silken cord surrounding the tailored waist of her *robe de chambre*. Her small hands twisted the dove-grey tassles, her long fingernails digging into her palms.

"No use wrecking this beautiful house of yours, " Magnus called from the bed. He beckoned her toward him, saying, "Many times it's better to share your problems. Come here. Tell me what's bothering you. Has your husband done something to upset you? Or is it . . . Abdee?"

Spinning in a rustle of silk, Anna screamed, "Don't talk to me about Richard Abdee. Don't talk to me about any man. I hate them all. I hate men! Hate them!"

He murmured, "You even hates me?"

Ignoring the harmless question, Anna resumed pacing the length of her bedroom, shrilling, "I might as well be a fat slave wench for all the liberty I get. Where's my husband? Out again tonight! At the Club Quadroon with his . . . mistress! But me! I cannot even be on the street with you! I would be labelled a slut. A whore. I would be tarred and feathered."

Magnus looked around the moire-walled bedroom, a chandelier twinkling in an ormolu mirror. He asked, "What's the matter with us staying here?"

"Here? You call this freedom? If my husband comes home and we're in bed together, I might as well . . . kill myself!"

"I thought you said he was at some club."

Anna fumed, "How can you depend on what a man will do? I hate men. I hate my husband and I . . . detest Richard Abdee."

"What'd Abdee do?"

"Do? I told him to keep those slaves till I collected them. I wanted to check around at other auction houses for current prices. My husband, of course, was not available to help me so the enquiries took me longer than I expected. Now this afternoon I learn that Abdee has up and sold all four hundred and twenty-five niggers! Sold them to Lynn and Craddock."

"Who's they?"

"Benson Lynn and Hiram Craddock, they own a so-called 'quality' auction house. They've always looked down their noses at me. They don't think a female should meddle in the slave trade. They've got some notion that Lynn and Craddock are superior to the rest of the world. And that's where Abdee went the minute I turned my back. Lynn and Craddock!" Gripping her fists again in fury, she said, "I told him to wait. To wait!"

Standing in front of a kidney-shaped desk, Anna picked up an ebony-handled letter opener and, stabbing it into a pile of papers, she threatened, "Well, Richard Abdee hasn't heard the last of me!"

Beginning to pace the room again, Anna slowly proceeded to form her revenge, speaking her thoughts aloud. "Abdee signed an agreement with us. Damn Hugh. He's got the documents with him. As soon as he gets home, I'll have those papers. I'll go straight to the authorities. I'll see that Abdee is kept from leaving New Orleans. I'll even see him locked in irons!"

Stopping suddenly in front of the Carrara marble fireplace, Anna motioned her hand toward Magnus to stay where he was. She had heard someone. A creak in the hall floorboards. She pointed toward the door.

Walking lightly toward the door, she reached for the brass handle and quickly flung the door open. She stepped forward and looked into the dark hallway. No one was there.

Rising cautiously from the bed, Magnus began to pull on his clothes. His heart was beating. He remembered Abdee telling him about white men castrating Negroes if they caught them with their wives. He did not want to live out his days as a free man with no testicles. What kind of freedom was that?

Anna kept standing in the open doorway, staring

158

down the hall. She called for her upstairs maid, "Lillibette? Is that you, Lillibette?"

No answer came.

Magnus was dressed now and standing behind
Anna. He whispered, "If you've got some snoops here,
I think it's best I go sleep back downstairs."

Anna was too occupied now with suspicions
about eavesdroppers to listen to Magnus or stop him
from leaving. She was looking down the hallway toward the carved railing of the main staircase, remembering how she had suspected lately that Hugh was
bribing the sneaky wench, Lillibette, to spy on her.

"*Lillibette!*" she screamed.

Still, no answer.

＊　　＊　　＊

The night air was warm and scented with roses,
lilies and bougainvillea vines which grew in profusion
around the white brick walls surrounding Oakbanks.
Magnus quickly sniffed the scented air and thought
how he would like to stay here in the right circumstances. Realizing that more than his manhood—
probably even his life—would be endangered by staying with Anna Tyler, though, he stood in front of the
moonlit wall and surveyed its height.

Before crouching to mount the wall in one leap,
though, he heard the crunch of buggy wheels on the
gravel path behind him, an avenue between oak trees
which led to the house. Magnus stepped into the
shadows and watched as the upstairs maid, the sober-
faced young black girl named Lillibette, stopped only
momentarily, at the gatehouse to whisper a few words
to the keeper. Then, as the keeper hurried to unlock
the tall wrought iron gates, Lillibette cracked a whip
at the dappled horse and disappeared into the Avenue
Bayou St. John.

Waiting for the burrheaded Negro to lock the iron gates and to return to the gatehouse, Magnus then jumped up the wall with one running leap. He reached inside his shirt when he landed on the ground outside the wall, feeling that his manumission papers were still secured inside the waistband of his breeches.

Knowing only vaguely about the direction he had to go, Magnus kept to the shadows of spreading oak and eucalyptus trees as he ran silently over the mossy earth.

He wondered if he was doing the right thing. He remembered how long he had waited for freedom, often believing that it would never come. Was he taking a risk by going back to Abdee? And what about Kinga?

14

CLUB QUADROON

Clouds of blue cigar smoke floated through the gracefully drooping fronds of palm trees planted in blue-and-white *cachepots*. Gay music tinkled from a raised dais where an orchestra sat in front of mirrored screens. Red-jacketed waiters moved through the sea of tables, agilely carrying silver trays loaded with crystal glasses and champagne bottles. This was The Club Quadroon, a rendezvous for affluent white gentlemen and their colored mistresses.

The young housemaid from Oakbanks, Lillibette, paused near the Doric columns flanking the pink marble steps which led down to the oval-shaped room. She glanced fleetingly at the orchestra and, then, drawing the hood of the black cloak around her face, she began to scan the crowd of people, anxiously looking for her master, Hugh Tyler, to tell him about his wife's activities with the free Negro, Magnus. Hugh

Tyler had promised to give Lillibette a gold eagle if she brought him news—at anytime, to any place—concerning his wife's infidelities.

The *maitre'd* approached Lillibette as she hovered nervously behind the Doric columns; he bowed to her, maintaining the Club Quadroon's custom of treating Negresses with the same courtesy and respect which white ladies received in other establishments in New Orleans.

Clutching the cloak further around her body to hide her slave smock, Lillibette quickly informed the *maitre'd* that she was looking for Mister Tyler, that she brought him urgent news.

The *maitre'd* answered "*Mais oui!* Monsieur Tyler is one of our guests tonight. He's with the charming Mademoiselle Chloe. Please follow me."

Clicking the heels of his patent leather boots, the *maitre'd* led Lillibette through the crowded tables to a corner where Hugh Tyler sat with a yellow-skinned young woman dressed in a white satin gown and wearing a shaft of egret feathers on the back of her elegantly marcelled coiffure. After a brief exchange of words, Hugh Tyler found a place for Chloe at a nearby table of friends and, then, escorted Lillibette quickly from the club.

*   *   *

"What are you doing back here?" Abdee was standing in the darkness on the starboard of the *Petit Jour* when Magnus dashed through a pile of wooden casks on the wharf and ran up the ship's gangplank.

"Anna Tyler!" Magnus gasped, breathing heavily. "She's going to have you arrested for selling the slaves to that other auction house."

"How do you know that?" Abdee held a bottle of

rum in one hand. Although he appeared to be sober, he reeked of the spirits. He did not greet Magnus with a smile, did not extend a hand to him.

"Anna Tyler told me! She's waiting for her husband to get home with some papers. She's going to have you arrested."

"You raced all the way here to tell me that?"

"Who else is going to tell you? You've got to leave . . . New Orleans!" Magnus gulped for breath, holding his stomach now.

"But I don't even own you, boy!"

Seeing the bewilderment in Abdee's face, Magnus said, "Hells man, I came to warn you. So instead of standing here on deck, we better get our asses ready to sail."

Abdee was thinking aloud. "Have me arrested . . . that does sound like something that bitch would do."

"Of course she'd do it. Now let's get moving."

"Can you help sail a ship?"

"Where's Pennington?"

"He's in his cabin still sleeping. His pansy boy's run off. Pennington's planning to go out looking for him again. If I wake him, he'll refuse to come. He'll want to stay here and I can't let him do that without getting another captain."

"What about Tewes?"

"He's pissed drunk with the sailors below deck. They've just come back from a new bordello. I was just thinking of going there myself."

"Forget about pussy! We've got to get this ship down the delta."

Lifting up the rum bottle, finishing the remainder with one gulp, Abdee tossed it into the water between the ship and the wharf. It splashed. He belched. He asked, "I take it you're coming with me?"

Slowly nodding, Magnus padded his waist band, "Me and my papers proving me a Free Man."

* * *

It was past midnight but Anna Tyler still could not get to sleep. She tossed restlessly on her silken sheets, wondering if she should creep down the back stairs and beckon Magnus up to her bedroom. She could at least calm her sexual anxieties by watching her reflection in the mirror as she worked her mouth to drain his masculine seed.

Hearing a creaking outside the door to her bedroom, she lay still. She listened. She wondered if she were imagining things. Or was that Lillibette lurking down the hallway?

Everything was silent now. Anna heard the alabaster clock strike one chime.

Repositioning the pillow beneath her head, she planned how she would go the first thing tomorrow morning to notify the port authorities about Abdee. She would definitely have him arrested for breach of contract.

Another noise attracted her attention. This time it was a floorboard creaking . . . inside the room. She had not even heard the door open. And, now, in a moment of panic she could not recall if she had locked it from the inside or not.

She called, "Who's there?"

Silence.

Raising her head from the pillow, she began to call again, "Whoever's there, I warn you . . ."

She then saw a figure, the outline of a man.

"Magnus?" she blurted.

As soon as she spoke the name, Anna knew that she had made a mistake. Why should she be calling out a black man's name in her bedroom? It was a confession of guilt.

Only then, when she saw the figure step into a shaft of moonlight streaming through the voile curtains, did she recognize her husband. Before she had time to call out to him, a blaze of light filled the darkness. Another pistol shot fired in the bedroom, its bullet tossing Anna's body farther across the bed.

Stepping across the shaft of moonlight, Hugh Tyler muttered, "Dumb, am I? A big, dumb farmboy? Well, we'll see how dumb I am, Annie old girl, when they arrest your nigger lover for killing . . . you!"

At that moment, Lillibette appeared breathlessly in the doorway of the bedroom. The hood thrown back from her head, she panted, "He's not there, Master Sir. That Magnus nigger done run!"

"Run," Tyler repeated. "Killed my wife, killed this lying bitch who's been calling me dumb all these years . . . he killed the lying bitch and then run . . ."

Facing the blood-spattered bed, Tyler said, "Good, I hope he runs all the way back to that God-damn slave castle where he belongs . . . I hope he stays there . . . I hope . . ."

Dropping his brace of pistols to the floor, Tyler slowly approached the bed and reached into his pocket. He withdrew a document from his pocket, the agreement he had signed with Richard Abdee to buy the slaves.

His eyes still focused soberly on the bed, Tyler began to shred the document, tossing the small scraps at Anna's lifeless body. The pieces of paper drifted slowly through the moonlight, falling onto the bullet wounds that had ripped open Anna's breasts, the paper particles soon blotting with redness as the blood continued to pour through Anna's negligee.

The light from the same moon glistened on the gulf stream, illuminating the full white sails of the *Petit Jour*. Abdee and Magnus took turns at the wheel, letting the ship luff, tightening the sails to breaking point against the growing wind, conning a course toward the Florida Straits. As members of the crew were woken from their drunkenness by the listing of the ship, Abdee left Magnus alone with them to explain the sudden departure from New Orleans. Locking himself in his cabin to avoid Pennington's wrath and the sailors' niggling questions, Abdee wondered what he himself had left behind in New Orleans. A family? A son held in slavery on a Louisiana plantation? He also thought again about that bordello named the "Petit Jour." Was the name more than just a coincidence? Although Abdee knew that it would be typically perverse of Naomi to call a bordello after his wife's plantation, he told himself that it could not be so. Naomi was dead. He had seen the room at Dragonard Plantation collapse in flames on top of her. And for his son . . . *I've had to make my own damned way in the world*, Abdee thought, *so let any son of mine do the same. I'm not going to get anywhere thinking about a damned son named . . . Pierre.*

Book Three

CARIBBEAN DREAMS

15

FRIENDS AND TRAITORS

The homeward journey from New Orleans logged seven days. The *Petit Jour* slowly eased through the gateway of *Castelo Novo Mundo*, the sails falling limp as the walls cut the winds which had carried the vessel into the enclosed harbor; the anchor splashed into the water, finalizing what had been an uncomplicated entry into the tower's center. But the sight awaiting Richard Abdee, Captain Pennington, Magnus and all the crew was not what they had expected to be their welcoming.

The plank doors, wooden gates, and iron grilles stood open around the sloping yard. The dirt appeared as if it had not been swept or raked for days; rubbish and driftwood lay scattered on the shore where it had been washed in through the open gateway from the sea.

Wooden shutters flapped in the breeze on the walls surrounding the harbor. A curtain hung through the open window of the dining-hall, the length of damask twisting down the hewn stones. Chickens strayed on the walls of overhead terraces which had been carefully latticed on the ship's departure for New Orleans.

Castelo Novo Mundo appeared as if it had been ransacked. There was no sign of human life, none of the raucous shouts or excitement which usually greeted Richard Abdee on his return from a voyage.

Abdee ordered the gangplank to be lowered from the ship's larboard side, its base thudding on the dirt yard. His footsteps echoed within the towering enclosure of the yard as he rigidly strode down the plank, holding one hand on a pistol tucked into the waistband of his breeches, the other hand gripping his whip. His eyes studied every shutter; he surveyed the gashes in the weathered walls which, served as windows; he scrutinized the doors, gates, and iron grilles.

Following Abdee down the plank Magnus also studied the disarray of open shutters facing the harbor. He heard nothing except the flapping curtains, the ebbing of the surf, the grunts, squeals and clucking of animals and fowl running wild. He had never imagined that *Castelo Novo Mundo* could look so abandoned.

Abdee stopped and stared at the iron gate which led to the Barracoon. Stepping closer, he peered down the stairway and saw none of the torches which usually flickered there.

Turning, he continued silently around the harbor until he reached the double door leading to the main entry hall. He jumped back when, suddenly, a pig ran squealing down the steps.

Abdee and Magnus stood side-by-side, both soberly surveying the emptiness of the vaulted and once richly decorated rooms. The Flemish tapestries were gone. The portraits of the Portuguese grandees were missing. An oaken table lay overturned on its side. The iron chandelier hung askew from a wooden rafter, its tallow candles littering the floor.

Abdee shouted, "Luma?"

As his voice reverberated against the stone walls, he next called, "Consuela?"

Receiving no answer, hearing nothing but the surf ebbing behind him in the harbor, he stared across the rubble at the circular stone stairway which led up to the dining-hall. the bedrooms and inner terraces.

He said to Magnus, "Everybody's gone—" He next looked to the pair of carved doors leading to the back entrance of the Barracoon. "—or dead."

Magnus asked in a hushed voice, "Was it pirates?"

Abdee shook his head. "Not here in the Windwards. Baptiste doesn't come this far south. Taubigny, Whibley, or Preacher Jack stay around Maracaibo for richer pickings. But even if it were pirates, how could they have got in the gates?" Abdee shook his head in bewilderment, still shocked at returning home and finding the portcullis raised but none of his people in the yard, no sign of anyone amid these shambles.

Taking a deep breath, Abdee's jaw began to work under his weathered skin. His cornflower blue eyes became dull as he began to think. Then, stepping forward to grab an unlit torch from an iron ring, he said to Magnus, "Start the men searching the entire place, I'm going down to the Barracoon to see the damage there."

* * *

After delivering Abdee's orders to Captain Pennington, Samuel Tewes and the crew of the *Petit Jour*, Magnus joined the search of the castle to find what further destruction had been done here in their absence, anxiously hoping to find someone hiding inside one of the rooms or towers, anyone who could explain the mystery of what apparently had been an attack and ruthless plundering.

Trudging up spiralling staircases, their stones worn into slopes by centuries of use, Magnus still found no clues. He wandered down dark passageways, searched room after room, climbed up wooden ladders to turrets. Discovering nothing except further signs of theft and vandalism, he began to draw a crude parallel in his mind between this inexplicable attack on the *Castelo Novo Mundo* and what he had lately noticed about Abdee's moody behavior.

Until Abdee's return from the last African voyage, Magnus had always considered him to be invincible, strong, as stalwart as this Caribbean fortress. He knew that Abdee was concerned lately about a lack of money. But the gold which Hiram Craddock had given him in New Orleans should certainly take care of that, Magnus thought.

No, what had first troubled Magnus about Abdee was not his desperate need for money, or his passion to resettle himself on a fertile plantation. The doubts about Abdee had begun when he had warned Magnus to stay away from Kinga. Conduct like that was not natural for a man usually so confident as Richard Abdee.

Wondering now if Richard Abdee was not as invincible as he appeared to be, Magnus wondered if Abdee said things which contradicted his inner feelings. Abdee always claimed that he loved no one. That he prided himself on being self-sufficient. Magnus wondered if this was true. Had Abdee loved that black wench whom he had lived with on St. Kitts? Was the memory of Naomi still haunting him? Was he trying to replace her with Kinga?

Slowly descending the spiral staircase to the Barracoon, Magnus held a pine torch which he had found lying in the debris of the dining-hall. He was still pondering Abdee's recent sullenness, wondering if he had made a mistake by leaving Oakbanks that night. He remembered how Abdee had been unable to comprehend that a freed slave would return to help him. Didn't he understand loyalty? Magnus wondered.

He stopped, hearing the echo of voices drifting from the darkness below him.

Listening more closely as he padded down the passageway, he heard a woman's voice answering a man's question. He recognized the man's voice as being that of Abdee.

Reaching a doorway, Magnus peered inside and saw Abdee crouching on the floor in front of a group of Negroes crowded into the dark cell. He saw Lolly Mumba, Moggy, Lisa, three Ibo guards, Pra, and a few of the other Ashantis whom Abdee had retained from the Tyler sale. Finally, he saw Kinga among the blacks. She had not been taken. He thanked God for sparing her and then quickly looked back to Abdee as the Negress in front of him resumed speaking. It was Luma and, as she crouched in front of Abdee and proudly held her precious bullwhip between her bent knees, she recounted what had happened at *Castelo Novo Mundo.*

* * *

The traitor, according to the story which Luma told, was Consuela. The half-caste cook arranged for the portcullis to be opened, allowing Claude Saint-Barbot's ship, the *Angelique,* into the harbor. He was the one who had plundered *Castelo Novo Mundo.* Consuela had been his accomplice. But, according to Luma's story, Consuela's strange actions had started long before that day.

"Consuela became a crazy woman," Luma explained to Abdee, "crazy and jealous. I found her one, two, three times sticking her finger down her throat to make herself vomit after she eats her supper. Only a crazy woman would do stupid things like that. Crazy!

"She don't stop looking at herself in every mirror she passes. She stands sideways, tugs at her clothes, grips at her waist. She starts acting like a crazy woman the very day you leaves here, Master Abdee, Sir. She sees me looking at her and she screams for me to go away. Ask Moggy there. Ask Lisa. They see her crazy in the kitchen. They tells you how crazy that Consuela turned. It makes me sad, too. Consuela and me, we used to be good friends.

"It's that Spanish blood. No nigger betrays her master like that Consuela do. She finds two Ibo guards with arms strong enough to crank the gate. She promises them prizes. Who knows? Maybe freedom. She says that her lover—her *lover!*—is coming back from Martinique. That her lover is coming to buy her and take her away!

"Lover! Ha! That Spanish pig has no lover! I *know* she's crazy. She vomits her supper every night. She lies to nigger men. She looks every morning out to sea. Ask Lisa there. Ask little Moggy. They sees crazy Consuela up on the perch like a hen crazy from some rooster, looking every morning for signs of his ship."

Shaking her head, Luma said that she wished that Consuela could see how the French sailors ran through the castle while she had gone aboard the *Angelique*. She complained, "That Consuela should be ashamed of herself. Them Frenchie sailors grabs silver and silks and tapestries. They crawls all over this place like a bunch of ants. I sees them do it before I rushes down the back stairs here. I sees them Frenchie sailors grabbing Eula, calling Eula dirty names because she's black. Like 'nigger whore' and 'mud hole' and 'black bitch.' But being black don't stop them pleasuring with her.

"I say 'pleasuring.' Ha! There ain't was no pleasure what that poor Eula got. I hid in the shadows and saw one Frenchie lift Eula up in his arms and bite her titties. Bite her titties hard right on the nipples. And when she tries to pound him on the head to stop, two men grabs her and holds her out in the air between them. Then a third Frenchie comes along and tells them to spread open her legs wide. Then he folds all the fingers of one hand together and starts sticking it up her pussy. It was awful. Eula screams like I never heard no wench ever screams before. And it weren't no pleasuring scream neither. I left when the Frenchie starts playing with his pecker with one hand as he's sticking his fingers folded in a fist up her pussy with the other. That's what kind of animal some of them Frenchies were. They rather screw wenches with their fists and beats their peckers with their hands rather than mount a gal like any normal man would do. That's when I thinks, 'Luma, you gets all the folks you can get together and hide them in this room faraway down here where them Frenchies don't see to come.' I thinks its best for some of us to be safe. I wanted to help save our house but I see what them Frenchies can do when they be left go wild. I guess poor Eula was one of the niggers they takes away with them from here. I'd rather stay here in this dungeon than go anyplace with some Frenchie."

Luma concluded, "I wish that crazy Consuela could see what she's done to our house now. I would like her to see the misery those French sailors left behind them. That Saint-Barbot, he used fat Consuela like a fool! No, never trust a fat girl. A fat girl will stop at nothing for love. Especially a fat, crazy girl with magic rosary beads. That's what brings Consuela's lover back here. The magic in her voodoo beads. That rosary. That's what gets a lover to come for a fat girl in a ship. Rosary beads! And a Frenchie's greed!"

❊   ❊   ❊

Word spread throughout the castle that night that the slave cook, Consuela, had betrayed her master by opening the gates to allow Claude Saint-Barbot to sail into the harbor and take her away with him to Martinique. No one doubted that the Frenchman had tricked the chubby young woman to believe that he was amorously interested in her when, in actual fact, he had returned only to plunder *Castelo Novo Mundo* in Abdee's absence. That Saint-Barbot had been angry that Abdee had not sold him the slaves. He stole the few he could find to salve his wounded pride.

Thomas Pennington held a different interpretation for the sacking of Abdee's stronghold. Although Saint-Barbot had carried away more than twenty of Abdee's slaves, as well as taking a small fortune in silver ornaments and cutlery, tableware, priceless tapestries, silk carpets, and oil paintings, Pennington believed that the Lord Almighty had prompted the theft and vandalism. That Abdee was being punished for sailing from New Orleans before Pennington had had time to find his beloved Robby. Had not the Lord predestined their meeting?

Set upon total revenge being wrought against Richard Abdee, Pennington saw Consuela's traitorous acts as the first step in the Almighty's plan for complete annihilation of Richard Abdee. Pennington hoped to share a small part in the next stage of destruction, to bring a merciless sinner completely to his knees.

Pennington, fortified with these crusading intentions, made his initial move of a carefully prepared plan. On this first night back at *Castelo Novo Mundo*, a time when the crew members' spirits were low, rumors spread among them that Abdee would not have money to pay their next wages, that he would spend the money which Craddock had paid him on refurbishing the spoiled castle. Pennington let it be known through Samuel Tewes that he had some money of his own which he might be willing to disburse among the crew at some future moment, a token for their eventual cooperation.

Leaving the crews' quarters, Pennington then descended deeper into the dungeons lying below sea level of the Caribbean. Armed with only a small pistol and carrying a wax taper, he headed toward the cell where he knew the Ashanti craftsman, Pra, was now incarcerated by Abdee. Pennington had recognized that Pra led a rebellious faction of Ashanti tribesmen and intended to include him in his plans for Holy vengeance.

It was not until Pennington crouched in front of Pra, looking at his gashed face in the candlelight, that he first felt frightened that the black man might overpower him, take away his pistol, and physically harm him.

Remembering the bond of friendship he had shared with Robby, Pennington told himself that he must forget the sinister tribal markings, to think of Pra as a human being enslaved by Abdee, some poor soul to aid in his misery.

He slowly explained, "I want to help you."

Pra narrowed his eyes, studying the English captain's corpulent body, scrutinizing his ginger whiskers, eyeing the pistol tucked in his waist band.

"I . . . like black people," Pennington explained,

pointing at his heart and then toward Pra. "I will help you become . . . chief."

Pra repeated the word. "Chief."

Nodding, Pennington continued, "Chief of all the black people. I have a plan for the black people. I like black people."

"Black people? You like?"

Knowing that he could have said /"loved," even "craved," Pennington glanced quickly toward Pra's crotch in the dim light. He remembered how often he had reached to fondle Robby's black masculinity.

Pra caught Pennington's eyes dip toward his groin. He smiled knowingly and nodded his head. He pointed at the bulk under his soiled loin cloth and then to Pennington. He said, "I know the white man's words. I know 'want.' You 'want' to help Pra so you can *have* Pra?"

Quickly shaking his head, Pennington said, "No, no. I have come here to be your friend. A . . . consort!"

Pra wrinkled his brow, asking, "Consort?"

"Allies. To be in alliance against Richard Abdee!"

Pra immediately understood and, as he leaned closer to listen, Pennington began to explain his plot, trying not to lower his eyes again to Pra's groin. He told himself that the Lord would not forgive him if he sought a sexual union with another man so soon after Robby's disappearance. The Lord would see it as covetousness. Pennington told himself that he must concentrate now on seeking vengeance. But he could not keep one thought from creeping into his mind . . . *Would I be happy with a man more mature than Robby, a black man old enough to be my rightful* . . .

He told himself to cast such thoughts out of his mind. He told himself to concentrate on destroying Abdee. He must force himself to mix more easily with the ship's crew and the black slaves before he began to reform his sexual tastes. He must keep his priorities in rightful order.

While Pennington's mind worked to organize his ambitions and desires, Pra also had secret thoughts. He smiled inwardly, knowing that the *greegree* still worked for him. Abdee had abandoned him to this cell. Had evidentally forgotten about him. If anything, Pra knew that Abdee would need him to help repair the damages done to this castle. What better time to seize the following days to regain leadership among my people, Pra thought, and also put this fat English captain to my use? The African gods finally were repaying Pra for being patient, for remaining faithful to age old beliefs.

16

LOLLY MUMBA'S CURSE

Richard Abdee immediately threw himself into the work of restoring order to *Castelo Novo Mundo*, beginning on his first night back at the castle by dividing the remaining slaves into work groups.

The next morning the gangs began cleaning the mess in the yard as well as the halls, rooms, planting terraces, and storerooms. There was not one corner of the castle which the French sailors had not spoiled, defiled, or uprooted.

While the slaves busily cleaned and made repairs, Abdee saw that he might as well seize this opportunity to whitewash the interior walls, replacing tiles on the roof, caulking holes between the stones where the wind often whistled in from the sea; he set about to restore the castle to a state far better than it had been when he had departed for New Orleans.

Another idea occurred to him, too, a plan to arm the slaves in case of any further attacks. Although he had given a large cache of weapons and ammunition to Ignatio Soto to trade with "Store Man" for the next cargo of African prisoners, Abdee still possessed a small arsenal which had been secreted under the stone flooring in the *sala de tormenta*.

The amount of time spent on repairing the castle took longer than Abdee suspected, though, and he had not begun to distribute the arms to the blacks. By the end of the first week, he had not even discussed the idea with Magnus.

It was during this first week back from New Orleans that Abdee realized that he had no peer with whom he could discuss his plans, either personal concerns or problems about the slaves. This fact had not troubled him before but the sacking of *Castelo Novo Mundo* had left an uneasiness in the atmosphere. There was little communication now between Abdee and the blacks. He did not know if it was his fault or if the blacks had somehow changed in their attitude toward him.

True to character, Abdee tried to force these suspicions from his mind. He had never before worried about his isolation among Negroes. He did not want to think about it now, the concept only adding to his load of burdens. He tried to persuade himself that his people still respected him, that their devotion had not changed.

Abdee rose early in the morning, thinking of the many chores he had to achieve throughout the day and, by nightfall, he was too tired even to consider pleasuring himself with a wench.

The only thoughts of female companionship which crept into Abdee's mind as he lay upon his mattress these nights were memories of his long-ago mistress on St. Kitts, Naomi. But he did not recollect their sexual rapport. He thought instead about the many hours they had spent discussing Dragonard Plantation, the slave quarters, the enormous difficulties of holding a small army of slaves in obeisance, and their hopes for the future. Richard Abdee fought himself these days from admitting that he was lonely for genuine companionship, that he somehow had mismanaged his private life.

He did face one fact, though. He admitted that if there was anyone in his life whom he had ever loved it had been Naomi. He tried to convince himself that he could easily exist without love. That he did not need love, a family, or close companionship. But if he had ever loved someone in the past, it had been that fiery Negress.

* * *

On one humid afternoon, ten days after the *Petit Jour* had returned from New Orleans, Abdee and Magnus worked together in the harbor yard. Abdee wanted to reinforce the strength of the iron gate which led down into the Barracoon. He strained with an iron bar to pry the bolts of the old gate from the stone archway, while Magnus swung a pick to make deeper holes to hold the posts of a new iron postern.

As Abdee and Magnus sweated side by side in the heat, Abdee began to explain his plan about arming the castle slaves.

Magnus disagreed. "You give a nigger his own gun and you're out for trouble."

Abdee applied more pressure on the rusty bolts, grunting, "If they had guns two weeks ago—we might not have to do this damn work now." The bolt came free.

Magnus continued, "It ain't the guns that would be protecting you. It's the attitude of the niggers who'd be holding them. You'd be taking a mighty big chance."

Wiping the sweat from his forehead with a soiled handkerchief, Abdee asked, "You're saying my people might turn against me?"

"What was that Consuela wench if she wasn't one of your so-called 'people'? She betrayed you didn't she?"

Considering Magnus's comment, Abdee finally asked, "What about you, then? I freed you, but didn't you come back to me?" This was the first time that Abdee had referred to Magnus's return.

"That's different, ain't it? I come back to you a free man!"

"Has your life changed because of your freedom? You're working harder than you ever did."

Magnus tapped the side of his head, saying, "The change happened inside here. I *know* I'm a free man. I *know* I can come and go whenever I want. And right now I chose to stay here. I likes working with you."

"Does that mean you'll stay here as overseer— even when I go to Martinique?"

Magnus, surprised by this sudden announcement, asked, "You going to Martinique? And leaving me in charge?"

"If you're so afraid these slaves are going to turn against me, you're the best man to leave in charge. It's not as if the job's new to you."

Wrinkling his forehead, Magnus asked, "Why you going to Martinique?"

"I can't let Saint-Barbot get away with this. And, besides, I want to get a look at his place there, *Côte Rouge.* I've got a few plans of my own."

"Now hold it a minute. Hold it right there. You ain't going to Martinique to do the same thing he done to you?"

"I haven't decided exactly what I'm going to do yet, Magnus. I'm just playing a hunch. Now stop asking me so many questions." He positioned his iron bar to pry out the next bolt from the wall.

Throwing back his head, Magnus laughed, confessing, "I must be crazy. I must be real crazy. It's crazy for a nigger to feel like this about a white man who owned him once but—"he looked at Abdee, admitting "—there sure is something about you I respects."

"You might not respect me so much," Abdee grunted, prying at the bolt, "if I told you everything about . . . Kinga."

Magnus froze at the mention of Kinga's name.

Stopping, lowering the tool, Abdee did not look at Magnus as he spoke. "I knew from the very moment you first saw that African woman you had eyes for her."

Magnus remained silent. He could not deny this.

"It made me mad," Abdee admitted. "I was determined to keep Kinga all for myself. So determined that . . . well, I just don't want her anymore. You've heard me talk about a wench I used to have called Naomi. That's who I want. But she's dead. And so—" raking one hand through his hair, he said, "—so, if you've still got eyes for that Kinga . . ."

"You saying . . ."

Abdee nodded. "I'm saying that if there's to be anything between you and that African wench, it's up to you to find out."

Magnus contained his happiness long enough to ask, "Something happened to you in New Orleans, didn't it? Something powerful?"

"Something did happen in New Orleans, Magnus. A lot of things. Apart from being at the mercy of that bitch, Anna Tyler, I heard something about my past, something about my family. A wife who's dead. And a son. The son's alive. Hell, I wish I would've heard instead about Naomi. But a man can't dream, can he?"

Soberly shaking his head, Abdee said, "I just don't want to talk about it. It's none of your business. I don't even want to *think* about it anymore. But you can do me one favor, though."

"You name it, Master Sir," Magnus said, addressing Abdee as he had done when Abdee had still been his legal master, saying the title now with respect rather than subserviently.

"Magnus, tell Luma not to come to see me tonight. I don't want to see Luma now. Not any wench. I want . . . I just don't want to see any wench. I don't want to think about anything except getting my feet on some good soil. That's what I'm going to concentrate on now. Finding me another plantation."

Although disagreeing with Abdee's philosophy of turning his back on love and dreams, Magnus only nodded his head. He knew better than to argue with a stubborn man like Abdee.

"And Magnus?"

He waited.

"Magnus, after you see Luma, go tell Lolly Mumba to come talk to me. Tell Lolly Mumba to come right away. And, then, just one more thing."

"Yes?"

"Don't go visiting that Ashanti woman till tonight. Stay out of the Barracoon till then."

Magnus agreed. He had waited this long. A few more hours did not matter.

* * *

Luma thought about the message which Magnus had brought to her that afternoon from Richard Abdee, brooding about it late into the night.

Master Abdee doesn't want to see me. He wants a rest. He doesn't want me.

Thinking about the words again and again, she tried to find a meaning, to decipher them into her own basic, simple terms.

Now, late that night, she sat alone in the light of a single torch flickering on the far wall of the *sala de tormenta*. She held the whip which Abdee had given her and stared down at its oily butt, remembering the many times she had used it as her master's phallus.

Thinking how stupid she had been, Luma angrily threw the whip to the floor, she buried her face in her hands, and as her mane of black hair tumbled around her arms, she began to convulse with tears.

What had happened to her life? Little more than a month ago, *Castelo Novo Mundo* had been wonderful. There were far worse places for a slave to live. Luma looked back to her wretched childhood in Maracaibo and saw this castle as a paradise. She realized now, though, that her contentment here had been solely due to Abdee having singled her out for his lover.

Lover?

Brushing away her tears, Luma laughed bitterly at the idea. *Lover?* What a fool she had been to think that the bond which had held them together was . . . love. Abdee used her as nothing more than his whore! His slave whore! He ridiculed her, slapped her, pulled her hair, sought sexual release with her with the same feelings as a . . . dog!

Abdee does not know the meaning of love, she thought, *I was a fool to think that he ever would.*

Looking blankly at the dark shadows in the room cast by a single pine torch angled on the wall, Luma wondered what future she had here. She had always planned that someday she would be Abdee's mistress, his lover, share a home with him like that Naomi wench had done on the island of St. Kitts.

Now, today, Magnus had brought the news that Abdee did not want to see her any more. She would have no future with Abdee at all. Who knew what would happen to her?

Her eyes fixed on the oily bullwhip lying on the floor, Luma realized that the leather tool had been far more satisfying in recent months that Abdee's manhood. The thick butt had done more than tease her sexual lips. She had felt the whip's butt inside her. Instead of a tool of torture as the whip had been made to be, Luma had used it for satisfaction. Fulfillment. Ecstasy.

Ecstasy! She shuddered. What kind of life did a woman have if she found ecstasy with a leather knob? Was it really fulfillment when a woman had to spread her legs, prod some object into her body, imagine that she was laying with a man?

Ashamed and depressed by her past behavior, Luma gulped back her tears and tried to obliterate the memories of satisfying herself with the whip butt. But the depression only increased. She remembered the many times that she had even spoken to the object, the moments of desperation when she lay curled in the dirt yard and talked to the leather knob as if she were speaking to Abdee himself. She had addressed words to it as if she were talking to Abdee's phallus. She had begged it for gentleness and love.

Sitting now in the *sala de tormenta*, she stared at the whip through her tears. She said, "You were the only thing I had to talk to. You were . . ."

She moved forward to touch it and, soon kneeling on the floor, she brought the butt of the whip toward her breasts and held it in her arms. She whispered,

"Foolish. Foolish Luma. To think that this is real. But this is my only friend. You is . . ."

Lifting the whip to her lips, she kissed its bluntness and whispered, "Help me. Oh, please help me find some different way now. Please. Help me end all this. I am so ashamed. Help me one last time."

Luma gently brushed the butt against her tearwashed cheeks, its oily length dangling down between her breasts, the leather coiled between her legs like a black serpent. She kept begging the whip to give her some sign or answer.

*   *   *

Lolly Mumba's gnarled brown fingers worked in the yellow light flowing from a wick dipped into a stone oil bowl. She knelt between Kinga's spread legs, wincing as she, first, separated the pubic hairs, then used a pair of small but sturdy pincers to snip the wires, trying to inflict as little pain as possible to the young Ashanti woman's tender skin.

Smacking her thick lips as she worked in the oil light, the ancient crone explained, "Master Abdee . . . he don't want these wires here no more . . . easy there . . . good thing he sends me and not that Pra nigger . . . Master Abdee tells me this afternoon to sets you free . . ."

As Kinga watched the old woman work with her sharp pincers, she listened closely to understand Lolly Mumba's words. Kinga had learned more than a few English words in the past weeks.

Lolly Mumba continued, "Master Abdee, he's like no other master. He treats us niggers good sometimes but—"

Stopping, she gently pulled out another wire, momentarily pressing her lips together, then saying as she worked to extract the next, "Master Abdee takes funny notions. Like you. He locks you together with wires. I thinks he done it to saves you for him. Now he says to sets you free. And you knows what I thinks?"

Resting back on her arms. Kinga tried to concentrate on the old woman's mumbling rather than to think about the pain.

Lolly Mumba delicately snipped another wire with the pincers, explaining, "I think Master Abdee lets that Magnus maybe visits you. Magnus, he's a good nigger but I learns he's a free nigger now. I don't know what freedom do to niggers. I never known no free niggers here. I tells you to watch that Magnus, pretty girl. I tells you to go . . . careful."

Snipping the same wire on the outer side of Kinga's vaginal lips, Lolly leaned back her head to allow the light to shine between Kinga's legs.

"Abdee's my master," Lolly Mumba said as she pointed the sharp tip of the pincers toward Kinga again, "but sometimes I think it's best for niggers only to trust niggers."

Kinga was too concerned with the wires being removed from her to answer Lolly Mumba. She knew too little about life here to agree or disagree.

Lolly Mumba said, "I learn things. The sky talks to me at night. I see blackness in the sky. Not the sky black. I see black people. But I don't know yet what that means."

Kinga asked, "You have magic?"

"That's all a slave can have," Lolly Mumba answered. "That's what hope is, pretty girl. Magic. But I see not just good magic happenings in this stone house built on this river with many streams."

The words made no sense to Kinga. She did not want to hear about magic. Pra had been preaching enough lately about traitorous devils among the black people. Kinga only wanted to be free from the golden wires before she decided who were devils and who were friends.

Lolly Mumba's hopes for the future, though, depended totally on omens and portents. She left the cell that night, telling Kinga to beware of bad magic surrounding her in the following days and weeks.

It was not until Lolly Mumba moved down between the sputtering torches in the passageway that she saw the first sign of what she considered to be bad magic. Noticing a faint light flickering in the *sale de tormenta,* she crept under the arched entrance to see who was in there. She suddenly stopped and gripped her throat. She started shrieking. The troubles for the black people had begun.

*   *   *

A knock on the door disturbed Abdee that night as he lay exhausted—and alone—on a cot in his tower room. He had been trying to decide on the day to sail for Martinique when Lolly Mumba rushed into the room as if a demon were chasing her.

Abdee grumbled, "What are you doing here? I told you to go to the Ashanti woman."

"Wires gone. Wires cut. I cut her wires. Then I leave her pen. I walk along the long floor. I look in big room and see . . ."

"Calm down, old woman."

Grabbing Abdee by the arm, Lolly Mumba begged, "Come with me, Master Sir. Come quick down under castle."

Abdee saw from the wildness in the old woman's eyes that something dreadful had frightened her. Tugging a shirt over his head and tucking it into his breeches, he followed her from his room and, soon, they stood side-by-side under the arched entrance of the *sale de tormenta*. He stared at Luma's naked body hanging from a wooden rafter.

At first, Abdee thought that a hemp rope was tied around Luma's neck but, walking closer, he saw that she had hanged herself by a leather whip, the same bullwhip he had given her as a symbol of authority in the yard. Luma had artfully tied the slick leather toward the tip of the whip into a knot and the thick butt dangled freely between her naked breasts.

Tugging at Abdee's sleeve, Lolly Mumba whispered, "The spirits always come now! The spirits always come to avenge the spirit of a woman to takes her own life, Master Abdee!"

Abdee did not at first hear Lolly Mumba's warning.

Jerking harder at his sleeve, she repeated, "The spirits always come to avenge the spirit of a woman who takes her own life, Master Abdee. You must burn a garter snake. Divide it into pieces and feed it raw to all those people who live under your roof. You must then write Luma's name in the dirt of the harbor yard. You must drop the blood of a freshly killed rooster into the sand. You must do all this very quickly, Master, Sir, or life here is not worth the bumps on a toad's throat."

Still staring at Luma's body creaking back and forth on the beam from the leather whip, Abdee felt the bile rise in his throat. She looked no bigger than a child.

Lolly Mumba jerked his sleeve a third time, whispering, "You must wrap Luma's body in bark. Tie it with green vines. Dump it in the water when the moon is shaped like a finger nail."

Pushing Lolly Mumba aside, Abdee threatened, "Stop that voodoo rubbish! Cut down the body. Burn or bury it. And then let that be the end of it."

Storming through the arch, he headed down the hallway, deciding that he would sail tomorrow for Martinique. He told himself that he must start looking for a place with fields, hills, solid earth, a place to breathe.

When niggers start killing themselves, troubles spread, Abdee told himself as he hurried past the wall torches.

He stopped. He heard footsteps descending the spiral stairs which rose from the end of the passageway. He next saw Magnus emerge from the archway.

Carrying a small parcel in one hand and a striped blanket folded across his arm, Magnus looked with surprise at Abdee. He was on the way to Kinga's cell. Despite the fact that Abdee had given him permission to visit Kinga tonight, Magnus felt awkward at being seen actually going there. He remembered how Abdee himself had been so obsessed with Kinga. He did not want to risk stirring any jealousy.

Brushing past Magnus, Abdee only said, "Lolly Mumba's doing some cleaning up in the big room. Don't bother her."

Abdee's words and clipped tone puzzled Magnus. He stood looking at him continue toward the stairs.

Without turning to look back at Magnus, Abdee called, "Get up to my room some time before dawn. I'm sailing for Martinique tomorrow. Remember, you'll be in charge here when I'm away. I want one last talk with you."

Then, he disappeared, leaving Magnus standing alone and confused, wondering what Abdee had been doing down here at this late hour. And why the decision to sail so soon? Also, why was Lolly Mumba doing chores down here at this hour?

Shaking his head, Magnus continued down the

passageway, deciding to mind his own business. Why risk the one chance for which he had been waiting?

* * *

Taking the piece of cold chicken and boiled turnip which Magnus had brought to her tonight in her cell, Kinga nodded her head in gratitude and then quickly began to gobble the food with a voracious appetite. She had not tasted fowl since she had left *Abidiri* on the slave ship.

Remembering how Pra had been recently cursing Magnus, condemning him for being a consort of white devils, Kinga decided that she could not hate this black man with the shaven head. She decided that if Abdee had freed Magnus from slavery, as she had heard, and this black man still had smiles for other blacks in slavery, and made their burdens easier, he could not be the evil man which Pra claimed he was. But Lolly Mumba had warned her, too.

Hearing Magnus cough, she raised her head. She saw him holding a cup of water toward her. He held a bottle in his other hand. He motioned for her to drink.

Gratefully taking the cup, Kinga gulped the water so quickly that it was not until she had swallowed the second cup more slowly that she realized that Magnus had tainted it for her with the juice of limes. She smiled. He was a thoughtful man.

It was not until Magnus held out a woollen robe in his arms, a blanket woven with red, yellow, and black stripes, that Kinga understood his intentions. He was wooing her.

She stared at him, this man with a shaven head, a Negro slave freed by his white master, a man who everyone said would be the chieftain here when Abdee went away. And here this same man was wooing her. Was offering her a blanket striped in red, yellow, and black.

Looking soberly at the African woven cloth, Kinga thought about her dead husband. This was the first show of affection in any form she had received since she had been carried away from *Abidiri* in chains. Would her husband's spirit forgive her if she accepted this man's polite gesture?

Magnus lay the blanket on the ground between them. Making no move to touch Kinga, he only continued to smile at her, his brilliant eyes twinkling.

Forgive me, she prayed to the spirits, then reached across the blanket to touch the hand of this free black man. The consolation of affection and love was more nourishing to her soul than food could ever be to her body.

They sat for a long time, Kinga and Magnus, holding one another's hands across the striped blanket until the time came for Magnus to leave. He slowly explained that Abdee was leaving tomorrow on the ship. That he must tell Abdee farewell. Then he would return to Kinga and they would find a room for her where she could see the sky, smell the air, feel the sun against her skin.

17

FORT ROYAL

The lush green hills of Martinique rose behind the portside of Fort Royal, climbing in a gradual slope to Mount Pelée, a now dormant volcano set against a cloudless blue sky.

The *Petit Jour* rested in the clear azure waters of Fort Royal's harbor, the ship looking drab and sea worn compared to the more brightly painted vessels whose masts and spars surrounded her on a softly capped sea.

Fort Royal now served as both the main port and capital of Martinique, presently a French controlled colony in the West Indies. A jewel-like island situated in the middle of the crescent of other islands stretching from Puerto Rico down to southernmost Trinidad off the northern coast of South America.

Richard Abdee did not yet know how long his business would keep him on Martinique. He ordered Captain Pennington and the crewmen to stay near the harbor, to venture no further than the native markets and thatch-roofed grog shops which made Fort Royal a colorful, relaxing community built on the edge of the Caribbean.

Like St. Kitts, Martinique had a history of both English and French government, the French now controlling the island, their official headquarters housed in a building which possessed much of the same flavor as the English headquarters in Basseterre.

Fan-topped windows lined the façade of the clapboard building which served as the Government House. Its interior was cool, smelling of parchment and leather boots, the humid tropical air circulated by a small black boy pulling a rope connected to a ceiling fan with rattan sweeps. Abdee felt as if he had momentarily stepped back in time, that he was in Basseterre, beginning his life afresh as a young man. The feeling of rebirth exhilarated him but, remembering that he was almost twice the age now of what he had been then, he also became agitated, anxious, wondering if he had regressed not only in setting.

This was not the first time in recent weeks that Abdee felt such uncertainties. He wondered if what some people called "luck" was now suddenly eluding him, or if this growing malaise was a toll of how he had led his past life. As usual, though, he tried not to question it. He looked forward, ahead to newer, stronger independence.

*   *   *

Presenting himself to the Director of Agriculture in Government House, Abdee stood in a high-ceilinged room, brusquely stating that he was interested in buying property on Martinique. He inquired about the schedules of any public auctions of sugar fields or farming estates seized by the French Government for non-payment of back taxes.

The official was a wide-eyed young Frenchman dressed in a white jacket decorated with blue fringed epaulets. He introduced himself as Alain Ribonne and made a few awkward attempts to ask why an Englishman should be interested in settling on a French island. He only referred fleetingly to the war behind England and France, inquiring in English about Abdee's past experiences in these colonies.

Abdee had decided to present himself only as a planter, to avoid the topic of his participation in the African slave trade. He answered, "I've lived in the West Indies for more than twenty years now. At present I live south of here in the Windward Islands. I own a small island not charted on any map. But the land there is not fertile. I desire to make a sizeable investment on an island like Martinique." He set down a metal cask on the Director's desk, an iron and brass box which contained the money which Hiram Craddock had paid him in New Orleans and the gold given to him on trust by Ignatio Soto to warrant their temporary partnership.

Trying not to eye the cask, young Ribonne began to stutter. Abdee knew that the Frenchman realized what the cask contained. Abdee was counting on French greed.

"Public auctions . . ." Ribonne shook his head. "I cannot give you any definite information about public auctions. But—" He hesitated. He foucused momentarily on the money cask. "—I *do* know there are a few tracts of land for sale on the island's western side. There's a tract of some ten *plats* which might interest you."

Abdee interrupted, "I want to invest in more than ten *plats*." He reached to lift the cask by its brass handle, saying, "I see I'm wasting my time and yours. I should be calling on a commercial agent." He turned to leave.

Rising quickly from his armchair covered in frayed brocade, Ribonne waved Abdee back, saying, "Wait, Monsieur, I just remembered a larger plantation . . . one with far more than ten *plats* . . . But to say that it would be for sale would be indiscreet of me. You could make enquiries from a certain banker here in Fort Royal, to learn if he's still holding a mortgage on it."

"I'm prepared to buy either mortgages or loans."

Sinking down again into his chair, the Frenchman said, "Ah, then I think you should see this . . . banker. His name is Monsieur Gerrard Ribonne."

"Ribonne? A relative of yours, Monsieur?"

The young official gestured nervously.

To put him at his ease, to clarify that he did not disapprove of nepotism, Abdee said, "I should be willing to buy the mortgage of any estate suitable for my needs. And to reward anyone giving me such privileged information."

Lowering his voice to almost a hush, the young Ribonne said, "We still have not established exactly what place you want.

"There is a plantation here called *Côte Rouge*," Abdee answered, staring him directly in the eyes. "*Côte Rouge* would suit me perfectly."

Ribonne feigned surprise. "How curious! That is exactly the place I had in mind."

Then, pulling out a pinchbeck watch from his soiled waistcoat, Ribonne asked, "Why don't you take a walk with me. I think I know where we can catch Monsieur Gerrard Ribonne at this very hour."

Together, Abdee and Ribonne left Government House, Abdee still carrying his cask of golden coins, and the young Frenchman making idle talk about sugar cane, the summer storms, the freedom from slave uprisings as of yet on Martinique.

Abdee kept pace with the quickly walking Frenchman, only slowing when he saw an elegantly dressed young lady seated in the back of an open carriage passing on the dusty street. He recognized something familiar about the dark-skinned female but, as she quickly pulled a lace shawl across her face and sunk deeper into the carriage, Abdee could not remember where he had seen her before. He continued to listen as Alain Ribonne explained that perhaps the three of them—himself, Gerrard Ribonne and Abdee— could ride up to the north end of the island to view *Côte Rouge* this very afternoon.

*   *   *

Abdee had been suspicious of the smooth-talking, oily-haired banker and entrepreneur, Gerrard Ribonne, when he had met him in his small office behind a coffeehouse in Fort Royal. But now as he sat astride a horse a few hours later, flanked by Gerrard Ribonne on one side and young Alain Ribonne on the other, Abdee stared down from a hillside view at *Côte Rouge* and ignored the banker.

Gerrard Ribonne had assumed control of the conversation since his nephew had brought Abdee to him. The three men sat on the knoll above the lush plantation, Gerrard Ribonne explaining that its present owner, Claude Saint-Borbot, would not take kindly to a future owner closely inspecting his property at this early stage of the bank's foreclosure.

The elder Ribonne then went on to explain how the soil on Martinique was enriched by lava spewn centuries ago by Mount Pelée.

Abdee still ignored his words. He gazed covetously at the fields rising and dipping below him, visualizing how he could develop this land into an agricultural estate to equal—if not surpass—the fertility of Dragonard Plantation.

Standing in his stirrups, Abdee saw that Saint-Barbot had not chopped back the jungle of vines and trees to make the most of his valuable property. That his cane processing mill stood in near shambles. Also, seeing the lines of rickety straw huts which formed the plantation's slave quarters, Abdee realized that Saint-Barbot spent most of his energy—and money—on the manor house.

Staring at the sprawling white house facing the sea, Abdee noticed how the driveway joined the house at a *porte cochere*, a porch supported by eight stately columns. A park ran from the front of the house down to the sea, a wide expanse of lawn which abruptly stopped at a stone wall where the ocean's waves crashed in majestic, thundering rolls.

As Abdree noted cannons placed at precise intervals along the retaining wall, their barrels facing out to sea, Gerrard Ribonne explained that *Côte Rouge* had been equipped years ago to defend itself from buccaneers. He drew Abdee's attention to a small pile of black balls piled next to each cannon. They were barely discernable from this distant view.

Abdee vaguely listened, continuing to gaze greedily down at the way in which *Côte Rouge* hugged the coast of the blue-green Caribbean, thinking that at last he had found his dream.

"Monsieur likes *Côte rouge?*" Gerrard Ribonne softly asked.

Abdee nodded. "Very much."

"We can return to Fort Royal?" Gerrard Ribonne continued, with a smile. "You would like to sign the documents?"

Abdee readily agreed that he would sign papers, anything that would make him the next master of *Côte Rouge*.

Turning his horse, Gerrard Ribonne called to his nephew and Abdee that they should ride quickly back to town at the south end of the island. He urged, "If Monsieur is lucky, we can reach my office before nightfall. Prepare the papers. Have a drink. Monsieur can find an inn. Alain can visit you there to conclude our business. Yes?"

Abdee was agreeable to any plan by this time.

*　　*　　*

Lying fully clothed that night on a bed in a room which he had rented in The Three Swans, an inn setting back from the bustle of Fort Royal's harbor, Abdee rested his head on a heap of down pillows and smiled with pleasure.

He was full of plans for the future, excited to clear land, rebuild the slave quarters, replenish its stock, improve the processing mill. He felt young, strong, brimming with hope. He even felt carefree for the first time in many years.

"Naomi," he said aloud, looking up at whitewashed ceiling, "we've got it, you black bitch! We've finally got ourselves another Dragonard Plantation!"

Laughing, shaking his head, he continued, "Oh, you called me your white nigger, Naomi, but, God damn it, I outlived you. I outlived you and landed on my feet again. Look at me! Soon to be master of *Côte Rouge*. So I guess a whitie isn't as weak as you always told me!"

A knock on the door abruptly disturbed Abdee's imaginary conversation. Rising quickly from the bed, he moved toward the door expecting to see Alain Ribonne on the other side. It had been intimated earlier at the office that the young man would come to the inn and collect a fee for introducing Abdee to his uncle. And Abdee planned to pay some small fee—gladly.

*   *   *

Consuela had been stunned to see Richard Abdee emerging that afternoon from Government House in Fort Royal. Although Abdee had stared at her seated in the back of the Saint-Barbot's teakwood barouche, Consuela was certain that he had not recognized her. Not after all the changes that had happened to her body and the extravagant wardrobe which now replaced the shapeless slave frock and long apron which she had worn at *Castelo Novo Mundo*. As she climbed the narrow stairway to Abdee's room at The Three Swans that night, she wondered how long it would take him to recognize her. She asked herself if she was doing a dangerous thing by coming here to see Abdee.

Lately, Consuela knew that she had taken many foolish chances. She fervently thanked the Madonna for helping her escape the trouble in which she had nearly landed herself regarding Saint-Barbot. *Ayal* Had she been wrong about him!

When Saint-Barbot's ship had appeared on the horizon beyond *Castelo Novo Mundo,* Consuela had thought that her prayers were finally being answered. That she had been right about Saint-Barbot's glances and romantic innuendos during his previous visit there. That he was coming back to the castle as he had promised, to take her away—yes, she was sure of it—to be his wife!

Consuela had felt no qualms about convincing the two guards from the Barracoon to raise the gate for her. She did not feel that she was telling them an outrageous lie by claiming that the *Angelique* was bringing a tempting supply of sweetmeats and fruit from Martinique. She knew that if a woman did not want to bargain with her body with men, she could usually get what she wanted by promising them tempting foods!

Having run hysterically to the harbor yard to greet Saint-Barbot, Consuela received her first shock when he told her in a polite, but not in the least romantic voice, to wait in his cabin aboard the *Angelique*. That he would join her momentarily.

It was not until Consuela heard the French sailors rushing from the ship, hearing the cries and shrieks echoing from within the castle, that she first suspected Saint-Barbot might have duped her. Even at that early stage, though, when she had been locked inside his cabin, Consuela still clung to the hope that Saint-Barbot had returned to *Castelo Novo Mundo* to abduct her for his lover. That soon she would be wearing a bride's white lace mantilla.

Claude Saint-Barbot did not pay his promised call on Consuela in the cabin throughout the entire voyage back to Martinique. Hearing voices which she recognized as those of black people from the castle, Consuela knew then that he had stolen the few slaves whom Abdee had not taken to New Orleans, even the two Ibo guards whom she had persuaded to open the gates!

Not being able to discern through the thick cabin door what valuables Saint-Barbot had also pilfered from the halls and rooms, Consuela heard the sailors laughing about the condition in which they had left the castle, the booty that they had claimed.

It was then that Consuela began to feel traitorous. Worse than traitorous! She felt totally responsible for the ignominious theft. She began to pound at the door, angrily shrieking to Saint-Barbot that he was a *"ladrón," "maricon,"* and *"merde"*—a thief, pervert, and excrement!

Her flames of anger had banked to a low, simmering fury by the time that the *Angelique* reached Martinique. They harbored to the south of *Côte Rouge* and, as armed sailors escorted Consuela across a sandy beach, down a jungle path, and emerging on a lawn surrounding a beautiful mansion, she still did not see Saint-Barbot—had not seen him since he had locked her in his ship's cabin.

Consuela's large brown eyes became wider, her temper subsiding, as she was escorted into the silk and velvet foyer of the manor house of *Côte Rouge*. A guard led her down a hallway smelling of bergamot, patchouli, and other spicy perfumes; he knocked on an ivory panelled door and motioned for Consuela to enter.

She stared in surprise at Saint-Barbot standing beside a bed. She saw a slim, grey-haired woman propped up on a mountain of pink cushions, one hand extending a warm welcome to Consuela, a smile spreading across her face—the face of an old woman who had obviously once been a great beauty.

Saint-Barbot said from his position by the bed, "Maxine, this is Consuela . . . Consuela, I want you to meet my wife, Maxine Saint-Barbot."

Still holding out her slim, pale arms to Consuela, Maxine Saint-Barbot said, "Claude has told me so much about you, *ma cherie*. Excuse me for not rising from this bed, but I do not walk."

Consuela stared from her, back to Saint-Barbot, then back to his grey-haired wife again. She looked at least twenty years older than the Frenchman. And what was she? A cripple?

Smiling, Maxine Saint-Barbot said understandingly, "You look so confused, *ma cherie*. Let me explain. It has been impossible to find me a companion. Claude told me that he had at last seen the right girl when he had gone to *Castelo Novo Mundo*." Smiling, shaking her head with pleasure, Maxine said, "And now you are here."

Not on that first night at *Côte Rouge*, nor at any time since then, had Maxine Saint-Barbot referred to the fact that her husband had stolen Consuela from Richard Abdee, along with the other slaves and many treasures. Consuela guessed, so far, that Maxine knew nothing about the matter.

Nor did Maxine explain as of yet why she was married to a man so much her junior in years. Consuela observed that the Saint-Barbots spent little time together except at evening meals and, then, conversation was always about life in France before the Revolution. Consuela slowly gathered that the Saint-Barbots no longer had an active love life. In the same token, though, Saint-Barbot made no amorous advances toward Consuela. She had been brought to *Côte Rouge* for the exact reason that Maxine had originally explained—to be a companion.

And to transform Consuela into a female suitable for a companion to so grand a lady as Maxine Saint-Barbot, the last two weeks had been filled with fittings for new clothes, choosing fabrics, making the right curls and marcels in Consuela's hair, plucking her eyebrows, and burying her face in cosmetic *masques*. A whole new world opened up for the slave girl and, now with all these luxuries at her command, Consuela was thankful that she had begun her special diet at *Castelo Novo Mundo*. After weeks of vomitting up her food, she was truly ready to be transformed into another person.

One of the most helpful hints which Maxine Saint-Barbot had taught Consuela was the experience of having a massage. The adept hands of a large black woman daily pulled and probed at Consuela's new body, firming the muscles, kneading the skin with turtle oil to obliterate any stretch marks on areas which not long ago had been flabby flesh.

Consuela had learned that the masseuse's expertise was what kept Maxine Saint-Barbot slim and healthy, giving her a far more youthful body than most women of her age. It was during Consuela's first days at *Côte Rouge* that she had first seen how the Frenchwoman could be physically fit without ever walking. She even learned why Maxine Saint-Barbot was always confined to a bed or chair.

Maxine Saint-Barbot was not infirm. She confided to Consuela that when King Louis had been removed from power in France by the Revolution, she had decided never to walk a step until her country was restored to a monarchy. Keeping true to her promise, Maxine Saint-Barbot never walked a step. She had servants carry her everywhere.

The black masseuse at *Côte Rouge* was yet another servant to help Maxine hold steadfastly to her resolution and cling to her health. The other services which the masseuse provided for her mistress were shown to Consuela, too.

Maxine Saint-Barbot invited Consuela ostensibly to watch her have a body massage but, seeing that the young black girl showed avid interest, she nodded to the large black woman to rub her hands beyond her thighs, to concentrate on the patch of brown hair between her pale legs. The black woman proceeded with her usual expertise, making the act appear to be more therapeutic than immodest and unnatural.

Watching the black masseuse working her hands

to gratify the sexuality of the slim-bodied French woman, Consuela was initially shocked. But when she saw Maxine's body soon contort upon the white-covered table in her dressing room, and remembering that the woman probably never made love with her arrogant husband, Consuela felt less critical.

Why should a female go without an orgasm? Consuela asked herself. Especially if she is married to such a cold, ruthless man.

Subsequently, Maxine told her, "We women must take care of each other sometimes." Although the conviction of Maxine's words removed any taint of sinfulness from the act for Consuela, she had not yet allowed the black masseuse do the gratifying act on her body. Consuela was still concentrating on beautifying her body.

Nevertheless, she felt a curious attraction to a camarederie between females. She was still sexually untouched by a man or woman, hoping to lose her virginity in a more natural way. What happened after that might be another matter. She did not know.

Mounting the stairs tonight at The Three Swans, Consuela debated with herself how much she should tell Richard Abdee. Or should she tell him any of what had happened to her? She knew that she was risking a happy future at *Côte Rouge* by coming here to see Abdee tonight. He was her rightful owner. But Consuela felt that she had to see him to know if she were making the correct choice—if a choice was even hers to make!

Despite all the changes in her life, despite the new luxuries she was discovering day-by-day at *Côte Rouge*, Consuela realized that she was still, by law, a slave. That Richard Abdee was her rightful master. She did not want to risk him finding her, dragging her back to the kitchen at *Castelo Novo Mundo*. She decided that it was better to approach him. To meet him on her terms.

* * *

Consuela could tell by the surprised expression on Abdee's face when he opened the door that he had expected to see someone else standing in the hallway.

She heard her voice brazenly ask, "Mister Abdee?"

Abdee nodded, smiling at seeing the dusky young lady whom he had noticed this afternoon seated in the back of the open carriage.

Stepping boldly past him into the room, Consuela tossed a pale blue silk mantle back from her raven curls, asking, "You do not recognize me, Sir?"

"Should I?" he asked, detecting an accent to her voice. What was it? French? Spanish?

"We knew each other in the past," she said, a twinkle now in her large brown eyes, her carmined lips puckering into a bow.

"I'm certain that if I had met a young lady such as yourself, I would certainly remember." He noticed now by the rich coloring of her skin that she might have Negro blood in her. He wondered if she was a quadroon beauty he had met years ago in New Orleans.

Gathering her gold skirt in one white-gloved hand, Consuela moved around the room in a rustle of silk. Her mind flashed to her recent past, the days at *Castelo Novo Mundo* when Abdee had completely ignored her. But—*Dios mio!*—she thought, look how he's ogling me now!

Encouraged by this change of attitude in Abdee, Consuela forced her cupid lips into a pouting expressing. She toyed with the pearl drops dangling from her ears, teasing, "You are certain you do not remember me . . . *Señor?*"

Bowing more gallantly than he had in years, Abdee reached for her gloved hand. He murmured as he kissed it, "Perhaps the young lady would like to refresh my memory?"

Disbelieving that the short-tempered tyrant she remembered from *Castelo Novo Mundo* could transform into such a charming person, Consuela began to have doubts about disclosing her true identity. She did not want to tell him that she was only Consuela, his cook, and see his gentlemanly treatment of her totally vanish.

Also, Consuela's original lusts for Abdee were flooding back to her. She remembered how desperately she had loved him, had waited for some sign from him that he felt the same for her. And now—*aya*—did she see it! His breeches bulged as if he had a piece of cook wood stuck between his legs!

Catching Consuela lower her eyes to his crotch, Abdee raised one hand to her shoulder and, pulling her towards him, he planted his mouth firmly on hers. His tongue then began to explore her mouth. He felt her breasts push closer against him. He had no doubts now that they wanted to share the same thing.

To Abdee's further surprise, the ravishing, dark young lady fell unashamedly onto the bed with him, their bodies interlocked as their kisses became more feverish.

Soon, Consuela's rich new clothes hung across a chair; Abdee's clothes sat heaped on the floor. They lay naked on the bed, Abdee softly working his mouth on Consuela's breasts; Consuela, keeping her eyes closed, brushing at his long, silky blond hair as she felt a passion she had only dreamt about.

She screamed and dug her nails into Abdee's back when he first pushed the crown of his swollen phallus between her legs. He realized by her gasps that she was still a virgin. He asked himself, *Who is this strange beauty?*

Inching more slowly into her now, Abdee treated Consuela with a gentleness which he could not remember showing any other woman. And with his excitement of deflowering a virgin, expecially a young maiden so beautiful—and eager—as the lusty female now passionately moaning under his body, Abdee soon crested toward an explosion. He could tell by the warm wetness inside her that she had undoubtedly already climaxed once and—he marvelled at her sensuality—was rapidly building with him again.

Finally, joined together like a fertility study of a man carved from ivory mounted atop the bronze body of a woman, Abdee and Consuela adhered together in a moment of mutual completion. Their cries became one. Her arms became part of his muscular back. Her spread legs overlocked his sinewy thighs. Her groin accepted the total thickness of his manhood . . . then they fell back together upon the bed.

They lay side by side for what seemed a blissful eternity to Consuela. Abdee's head cradled in her arms as she slowly ran her fingers through his perspiration soaked hair.

He murmured about her virginity, "I must not have known you very well."

She had no power now to withhold anything from Abdee. She answered, "I am Consuela."

There was a pause. He slowly repeated the name, "Consuela?"

She felt his naked body stiffen next to her.

Continuing to finger his hair, she said, "You have every reason to be angry . . . Master Abdee. But if I hadn't done what I did, then we wouldn't have had this experience, no?"

His voice instantly became hard, threatening as he asked, "Where is he?"

"Claude Saint-Barbot? He's probably with his wife."

Abdee raised his head with a jerk. "His wife?"

"*Si!* He's married. Saint-Barbot is not my lover."

"But you . . . Luma said . . ." Abdee was now seated naked on the edge of the bed. Staring at Consuela, he could definitely see a vague familiarity between this sensuous young lady and the half-caste slattern from *Castelo Novo Mundo.* Beginning to shake his head, he said, "No, I cannot believe this!"

"What? That I am no longer fat? Or that Saint-Barbot is married?"

"But you let his ship into the harbor!"

"Ah, that! I do not deny I was a fool. I am not trying to deny that. But neither am I asking you to forgive me. I can explain why I *think* he lied to me. I can tell you that."

"Stop, I don't want to hear any more of this. Not now."

Running her finger up his knee, Consuela purred, "Good! I'd rather talk about you. Tell me please why you are here in Martinique." Her eyes twinkling again, she asked, "You did not come all this way to find little, fat Consuela?"

Abdee was in no mood for jokes now. Especially from women who were rightfully his slaves. He said, "Wait until tomorrow. You'll see at *Côte Rouge* why I came to Martinique."

Standing naked from the bed, he ordered, gruffly. "Put on your clothes. It's a long ride home. We'll talk about your future tomorrow."

Not wanting to go yet, Consuela asked in her

new assurance, "But tell me a little news about . . . home. How is Luma?"

"Luma's dead. She killed herself."

The announcement stunned Consuela. She gasped, "Dead? But why?"

"How do I know why? She hanged herself in the Barracoon, damnit. I sent word that I didn't want to see her any more and the next thing I knew . . ." Raking his crooked fingers through his hair, Abdee shouted, "Put on your clothes. Stop asking me all these questions. Get out of here."

Rising slowly from the bed, Consuela moved in a dazed state toward the chair that held her clothes. She thought soberly, *Luma's dead . . . because he didn't want to see her any more . . . she killed herself for him . . .*

Consuela dressed herself slowly, slipped into her new calfskin slippers, gently rearranged her hair. She did not speak to Abdee as she did all these things; she was remembering how jealous she had once been of that poor, short slave girl called Luma. And now, here she was—fat Consuela—slim, artfully coiffured, dressed like a proper lady, with a barouche waiting to drive her to the finest plantation on Martinique. But Luma? Luma was dead. Consuela could not hold back the tears which began to trickle down her face for that little . . . *puta de Maracaibo.*

*   *   *

Thomas Pennington could not remember ever having bought drinks in a grog house for anyone but tonight, the crew's first night in Fort Royal, Pennington insisted that the innkeeper at a harborside house provided drinks for everyone from the *Petit Jour*. And as the innkeeper began to carry the brown coconuts to the raucous crew crowded into the thatch-roofed establishment, Pennington forced himself to praise the island's favorite drink—rum generously mixed with the fresh milk of a coconut.

Pennington urged the rowdy men to drink more, saying that he wanted his men to start enjoying themselves. He insisted that they spent too much time locked up in their bleak quarters at *Castelo Novo Mundo*. He told the mixture of Irish, Scots, Welsh, and American seamen that a sailor's life was meant to be spent at sea. But, still, Pennington did not know how he was going to broach the subject that, some day in the very near future, he was going to ask them to offer their assistance to a certain group of black people. Pennington knew that it would take more than rum-spiked coconut milk to make these particular white men forget their prejudices against black people. Pennington's plan to annihilate Abdee, though, totally depended on these sailors' agreement to turn against a white man in favor of some blacks. Shouting for the innkeeper to bring yet another round of rum to the tables, Pennington decided to begin stirring discontent about Abdee's failure to pay the crew their wages—that if it were not for their captain's generosity, they would not be drinking rum from coconuts, but wandering the harbor of Fort Royal like the Caribe Indians, using coconuts for begging bowls.

18

COTE ROUGE

Abdee awoke in a foul temper the next morning, not
knowing if he was more furious at Consuela for securing Saint-Barbot's entry into the harbor at *Castelo
Novo Mundo* or for withholding her true identity from
him last night until after they had finished making
love. He still felt his manhood harden when he
thought back to last night. Nevertheless, he had to
think of some way to reprimand Consuela once he became master of *Côte Rouge*. He could not allow a
slave wench to cavort around a plantation in fancy
clothes, spreading rumors how she had fooled her
master.

Putting Consuela's future momentarily out of his
mind, Abdee dressed and went from The Three Swans
to Government House. Young Alain Ribonne had
promised to give him the last papers today which
proved ownership to *Côte Rouge*. Also, there was still
the matter of paying the introduction fee. After pre-

senting the papers to Abdee, though, and covertly accepting the gold for introducing Abdee to his uncle, Alain Ribonne sat behind his official's desk in Government House and asked Abdee what he was planning to do about back taxes. The outstanding amount due to the French Government equalled the price of the property itself.

Trying to suppress his anger, Abdee asked, "Why did you not inform me about taxes yesterday?"

"But Monsieur, you came here mentioning taxes. I thought you had taken that into consideration. It was no secret. We only went to see Gerrard Ribonne to buy the mortgage held against *Côte Rouge*. Gerrard has nothing to do with taxes. He is a banker. The taxes comes from the Government."

Abdee could find no way to argue with that. He immediately saw his fault of accepting the banker's terms too quickly; he reddened at the thought of acting so compulsively, not to have weighed the fact of a Government's loan.

"How long do I have to pay?"

Again, full of courtesy and respect, Ribonne answered Abdee, "You will be given a decent amount of time, of course, Monsieur. We still have to notify Monsieur Saint-Barbot about the foreclosure."

"At least give me that pleasure!"

Beginning to shake his head, Ribonne said, "I am afraid that is not regular . . ."

"It is not regular for a man in your position to accept bribes either!"

Quickly motioning with his hands for Abdee to lower his voice, Ribonne glanced toward the louvred doors to make certain that no one had overheard the crass remark. He quickly capitulated in a near whisper, saying, "Fine. I see no difficulty about you telling Monsieur Saint-Barbot that you are the new master of *Côte Rouge*. I see no reason at all."

Abdee stormed from Government House more angry at himself than the nepotism of the Ribonne nephew and uncle. The mistake was his. He had always prided himself on facing his own blunders. And he knew that when he made them, they were colossal. He had no doubts, though, that he could raise money to pay the taxes. Astride the mare, he had already devised how he could sell all the contents of *Côte Rouge* if necessary. *Hell! Half are mine, anyway*, he thought. *Carried away from* Castelo Novo Mundo *as booty!*

Although wanting to head immediately toward the north end of the island, Abdee galloped instead toward the harbor. He had to alert Pennington and Tewes to gather all the crew members aboard the *Petit Jour*. Abdee wanted them to catch the wind as it was building, to sail from Fort Royal to a cove adjoining *Côte Rouge*. He wanted them there by sundown. He hoped to be there much earlier himself.

And I must remember to warn them about those bloody cannons. I wouldn't put it past that French bastard to fire on my ship, too. I must remember to remind Pennington to stay well to the south. No. I'll tell Tewes. Pennington's still acting too stupid over losing that nigger pansy boy.

* * *

Consuela awoke that morning in her bedroom at *Côte Rouge* with the ominous feeling that something dreadful was going to occur today. She quickly dressed herself in one of the frocks of pastel dimity which had been made for her to wear at home.

Going to join Maxine Saint-Barbot in a walled section of the gardens, Consuela was surprised to find that she was not there. Tobias, the butler at *Côte*

Rouge, informed Consuela that Madame Saint-Barbot was breakfasting with her husband and would most likely be with him until midday.

Maxine Saint-Barbot did not join Consuela in the garden until the middle of the afternoon. Two husky black men, Titus and Coro, walked slowly along the flagstone path, their hands joined together to form a mobile chair on which Maxine sat, an arm placed around each of the black men's necks. They proceeded toward a cluster of garden furniture and, as Consuela rushed to pull back a blanket, the two men lowered their mistress onto her garden day bed.

Settling herself on the cushions, Maxine Saint-Barbot asked Consuela if she would join her in a glass of chilled mint tea and, while Tobias went to fetch it, Maxine explained why she had been detained so long with her husband.

"Claude's not a very competent manager," Maxine said, leaning her head back on the glazed cotton cushions, a few strands of her grey hair fluttering around her face as she fanned herself with a semi-circle of parrot feathers. "He's having financial troubles again. Rather serious ones this time. I know it's indiscreet of me to tell you this, *ma cherie,* but it might help you to understand your future here—" She paused, staring at a potted yellow poinsetta, saying blandly as if speaking to herself, "—if there is a future for any of us here at all . . . thank God I bought that cottage in Fort Royal!"

Kneeling on the grass beside her bed, Consuela explained the strange feeling of foreboding which she had had this morning.

Maxine replied quickly, but not maliciously, "Perhaps it's because of your visit last evening to Fort Royal, dear Consuela."

Consuela stared at her. Although not knowing

how much Maxine knew about her visit to The Three
Swans, Consuela could not lie to her. She already felt
indebted to this stately woman. She lowered her head,
confessing, "Yes, it is because of my visit to the inn.
You see, Master Abdee . . . he is on the island."

The cosmetic *môle* on Maxine Saint-Barbot's chin
slightly quivered as she stared with horror at Consuela. But her voice was calm as she inquired, "Has he
come back to claim you, *ma cherie?*"

Consuela froze. So Maxine *did* know that her husband carried her away illegally from *Castelo Novo
Mundo.*

Reaching for Consuela's hand, Maxine said, "I am
not as sheltered as many people think. I depend on
spies for much of my knowledge. I know exactly what
misdeeds my husband did at *Castelo Novo Mundo.*
Claude told me that he went back there to collect
some slaves that he had bought from this Englishman,
Richard Abdee. He told me that he had found a
lovely Spanish girl, a young lady who, with a little
work done on her, would make a lovely companion for
me. Claude has a good eye for spotting rough dia-
monds. But I later learned that he had actually stolen
you, along with other slaves, as well as looting the castle. I then understood where he obtained all those
new treasures still sitting in our foyer. Claude is very
avaricious. That is why he married me, a woman almost twice his age. He saw what I could give him.
And I . . . I love youth!"

Looking benignly at Consuela, Maxine proceeded, "I also learned that caddish manner in which
my husband tricked you into opening the harbor gates
there. Claude has always had a devious nature but,
sometimes, I swear, he has become more evil. That he
has changed much since I married him. My own fortune has dwindled since he met me but his desire for

luxuries has increased. Alas, he is not mentally equipped to build a new fortune. His attempts at growing sugar here were totally disastrous. Then he decided to go into slave trading. When that failed, he slowly began to turn into a . . . maniac. I barely recognize him any more. The only comfort I get is from our home here. I love *Côte Rouge*. But now Claude tells me . . ." Her eyes misted with tears; she studied her clutched fingers. ". . . now Claude tells me that he owes money on *Côte Rouge*."

Stopping, trying to choke back her tears, Maxine said, "The only thing I truly cherish in the world is *Côte Rouge*. It has been our only home since we fled here from France. It is almost like a child to me, something Claude and I planned and built together. I will do anything, *anything*, rather than see him lose it to a bank or another man. I would destroy it first. Destroy it! I would rather die along with it, rather than . . . ," she bent her head, sobbing.

Rising on her knees to console Maxine Saint-Barbot, Consuela said, "You will not die until the Lord chooses to take you. And that certainly will not be here! What about that cottage you have in Fort Royal? If Claude is too grand to live there, I will take care of you!"

"You are very kind Consuela. Very understanding. I would love nothing better than that. But—" she shook her head, "—you are owned by another master."

"Abdee is like no other master," Consuela began to argue, "I know him! And perhaps if I asked him to sell . . ."

Maxine interrupted, "Are you in love with him?"

Consuela hesitated then, shaking her head, she answered plainly, "I have learned much about love. You have helped me to discover myself. To appreciate myself as a woman! And I want to learn how to live to the hilt before I make any choices in love. The only thing I know is that I want to serve you. I am willing to do anything. Cook for you. Clean. Be your companion. Even give you your daily . . . *masaje.*"

Reaching forward, Maxine beckoned Consuela to take her hand. She asked in a quiet voice as the girl held it, "Would you kiss me . . . Consuela?"

Consuela looked directly into Maxine's eyes. The request did not shock her. She understood the words completely. If anything, they were what she wanted in her heart to hear. Leaning forward, Consuela closed her eyes and brushed her lips gently against Maxine's, tasting a sweetness she had never known before, a tenderness she had not felt from Abdee last night.

Feeling Maxine's hand fall onto her breast, Consuela pushed herself forward, moving her tongue around Maxine's mouth, feeling now both love and security in the embrace. She had discovered sexual ecstasy with Abdee last night, true, but this tenderness was all new, and far more welcomed.

Finally forcing herself to pull back, Consuela whispered, "Do not misunderstand me. I do not pull away from you because I want to stop. But I gave you my devotion and I must remain true to my words."

"I can tell you have something very important to tell me, *ma cherie.*"

Consuela nodded. "A warning. A warning about Richard Abdee. I know that he means to seek revenge against your husband for attacking *Castelo Novo Mundo* in his absence. I do not know how Abdee means to strike back but I fear it might be against your home. Against . . . *Côte Rouge.*"

"He will not succeed. No one will touch nor possess *Côte Rouge* except me!"

Consuela warned her, "Richard Abdee is very

strong. And vindictive! I am afraid if he confronts your husband, Abdee will win. Also I know that Abdee has gold from his slave sales. Gold makes men powerful!"

Patting Consuela on the head, Maxine said with renewed conviction, "Muscle and gold are no match against the wiles of a woman. And there are now two of us."

Flinging herself on Maxine, Consuela promised, "I will serve you faithfully. *Por siempre.*"

Hearing the sound of galloping on the driveway beyond the walled garden, Maxine Saint-Barbot said, "I think our guest is here. Quick, run and get Titus and Coro. If what you say is true, Consuela, we must act very fast."

Consuela looked at her quizzically.

With courage in her voice now, Maxine said, "Confident that I have you to help me in the future, I will carry on with my convictions. No one will take *Côte Rouge*. If I cannot possess it, then no one will."

Maxine quickly proceeded to explain a plan to Consuela, urging her to run now and organize a few trusted house servants into groups by the cannons along the sea wall. Telling her also to order Titus and Coro to come immediately to the garden, Maxine said that they would meet in the carriage house. They would escape together to Fort Royal.

* * *

The sun was sinking into the Caribbean horizon, streaking the sky orange and purple as Abdee galloped toward the white-columned *porte cochere* of *Côte Rouge*. His irritation at arriving here so late now disappeared when he saw the lean figure of Claude Saint-Barbot emerging from the house.

Dressed in white breeches and a ruffled linen

shirt, Saint-Barbot did not wear one of his many brocade jackets, nor his dandy's wig. His dark hair was pulled back into a knot at the nape of his neck; his nose, his bright green eyes, his firmly set mouth, gave him a hawklike determination. He positioned one hand on his hip, motioning down the driveway with the other, calling to Abdee, "This is my land. I order you to leave. Come no further!"

Abdee dismounted his horse and taking a whip from the saddle, he called, "I'm afraid you're wrong. I have a document here to *prove* you're wrong! And if that does not convince you . . ." Abdee unfurled the whip, its splayed tip snapping in the air.

Backing into the house, Saint-Barbot sneered, "Your barbaric conduct does not surprise me, Monsieur . . . Dragonard. I see you are no gentleman."

Suspecting that Saint-Barbot was merely stalling for time, Abdee proceeded toward him, replying, "And I suppose you behaved like a blasted gentleman by sacking my home when I was away. Stealing my people. Leaving the place in a shambles." He snapped the whip again to punctuate his anger.

Saint-Barbot stood between the open doors which led into the foyer, a few servants scurrying quickly behind him, abandoning their evening duties of preparing the house for the night when they saw a stranger force their master into the house with a whip.

Abdee called, "It was you, too, Saint-Barbot, who set fire to the *Southern Zephyr*. You're a model gentleman, aren't you!"

"You come ready with outrageous accusations, Monsieur," Saint-Barbot answered. Then, reaching inside the door, he suddenly withdrew a rapier and jumped forward, jabbing its steely point toward Abdee.

Quickly side-stepping the thrust, Abdee drew

back his hand to lash the whip again but, before the leather snapped, Saint-Barbot jumped forward and sliced Abdee across the forearm with his rapier. The whip fell to the floor.

Holding his arm with one hand, Abdee reacted by sticking out his booted foot, tripping Saint-Barbot as he rebounded from his sword thrust.

The Frenchman fell forward, his rapier clattering onto the marble floor, and as Abdee jumped on him, the two men began to grapple in the foyer, blood from Abdee's arm now beginning to smear across the polished white marble floor.

Lying astride Saint-Barbot now, Abdee gripped his strong fingers around the Frenchman's neck, clenching hard to break his windpipe, his own blood streaming down onto his hands and Saint-Barbot's neck.

His face coloring from loss of breath, Saint-Barbot choked as he strained toward Abdee, digging his long fingers into Abdee's eyes, trying to force both eyeballs from their sockets.

Pulling back his head, Abdee heard a crash behind him. Hearing crystal shatter on the floor, he did not know what he had knocked over until he saw the candle from a hurricane lamp setting fire to a *moire* cloth covering the foyer table.

Then, a second shock was added to Abdee's horror as he looked across the spreading flames and saw a heap of silver candlesticks, golden chalices, tapestries, and portraits of Portuguese grandees heaped nearby in a corner—the booty from *Castelo Novo Mundo*.

Gaping at the valuables, looking at how the arrogant Portuguese faces seemed to be sneering at him through the leaping flames, Abdee realized that he somehow must drag them from the house if he had to redeem them for cash to pay the land taxes.

That instant flash for survival, though, was interrupted as Saint-Barbot came lunging toward him, toppling Abdee backwards onto a rosewood spinet.

Locked again in a struggle, the two men gripped at one another, each trying to withdraw an arm to drive a clenched fist into the other's face, chest, or stomach.

As Abdee kneed Saint-Barbot between the groin, the Frenchman clung to him and they tumbled along the keyboard of the spinet, their weight making the piano fill the foyer with banging, jarring, atonal sounds.

It was at that moment that a second noise thundered around the two fighting men. The entire house shook with its impact.

* * *

Consuela screamed at the house slaves, reminding them that they were following their beloved mistress's orders by turning the cannons from the sea and firing the balls against the manor house.

Seeing the gash made in a wall by the first aim, Consuela ranted for the second group of slaves to light the fuse and set off the next volley. Maxine Saint-Barbot wanted *Côte Rouge* totally reduced to rubble.

The sudden explosion in the manor house caused immediate turmoil in the nearby slave quarters. Consuela could hear the pandemonium as the black slaves ran screaming from their thatched huts.

Shrieking at the black men positioned at each cannon, Consuela commanded them in a mixture of Spanish, English and French. "Fire again, *mestizos!*

Fire! *Comprennez-vous?* Destroy the house! Destroy it!"

A second, then a third and fourth boom filled the air in quick succession. The force of the cannon blasts hurled Consuela back onto the ground. She raised herself and saw through a cloud of blue smoke that the slaves had abandoned her, that they were scattering through the forest and fields with the people from the slave quarters.

As the cannon smoke began to lift above the lawn, though, Consuela saw flames rising from the house, black smoke belching from the windows in the few remaining walls.

Although knowing that her mission was completed, Consuela felt a sharp pang inside her breast when she remembered that Abdee was somewhere in that growing inferno. Had she killed him?

Remembering the decision that she had made when Maxine Saint-Barbot had proposed this idea to her only a short time ago, Consuela quickly sprang up from the ground. *Aya!* Abdee! *He got tired of Luma and she killed herself! Not me! Consuela wants to . . . live!*

Quickly gathering the soiled and ragged hem of her skirt in one hand, Consuela brushed the hair from her sooty face and rushed across the lawn toward the carriage house.

* * *

A wax taper flickered inside a crystal hurricane lamp, causing the posters of a brass bed to cast long shadows across the floor of a small bedroom in a cottage built along the quay of Fort Royal. Two naked women lay upon the bed, the light skin of one woman contrasting softly against the dusky sheen of the other as they held one another in a tight embrace.

Consuela lay on top of Maxine Saint-Barbot. Raising to lick the rosy nipples of Maxine's small breasts, Consuela soon worked her tongue down toward her slim waistline, smoothing Maxine's milky skin as she listened to her gasps become louder, more excited.

Lifting herself, Maxine reached toward Consuela's naked shoulders. She pulled her toward her. She held Consuela's face between her hands, kissing her forehead, eyes, cheeks, and lips.

She whispered, *"Ma cherie, ma cherie,* I do not want our love to be one-sided. I want to satisfy you as—"

Raising one finger to her mouth, Consuela said, "Shhh. We have years. We have a lifetime ahead of us for you to enjoy my body. For me to make love to— look at the beauty you keep hidden beneath your clothes! As you taught me certain secrets, I will help you, too. Who knows? I maybe even will get you to come walking with me . . . just the two of us."

Then, moving her breasts across Maxine's face, Consuela pressed one nipple toward her mouth as Maxine reached to fondle the other breast with her hand.

Quickly turning herself around on the bed, Consuela straddled her black patch of hair over Maxine's face and bent down over Maxine's stomach to take her brown patch in her own mouth.

Both females soon hungrily worked their tongues on one another's femininity. They had completely forgotten about the cannon explosions and fire which less than a few hours ago had destroyed *Côte Rouge.* They concentrated now on a life in which no man—as husband, lover, or master—had a place.

19

THE AFRICAN BLANKET

Magnus wrapped his arms around Kinga's sleeping body, luxuriating in the touchings of their nakedness, feeling the happiest he had ever felt in his entire life. Three days had passed since Abdee had sailed for Martinique, this being the third night that Magnus and Kinga had slept together in the tower room.

Despite the grey bleakness of this once richly furnished bedroom, Magnus knew that he would not recognize these quarters even if they were still furnished in their former splendor. This was the same room in which Anna Tyler had slept, had looked at herself in the cheval mirror as she knelt on the floor in front of Magnus's naked body. But Kinga's presence here transformed the room into an entirely new place for Magnus. His world at *Castelo Novo Mundo* had completely altered since Kinga had given him her friendship. This was the meaning—one genuine meaning—of freedom. Love. Not yet a consummated physical "love" but an unspoken understanding between Magnus and Kinga which made him feel proud and truly free.

On their frist night together here, Magnus sensed that Kinga was questioning his motives for taking her from the Barracoon, and bringing her up the spiral steps to a room furnished with nothing but a straw pallet. Magnus saw from the terror in Kinga's eyes that she still expected an ulterior motive to his generosity.

To place the frightened woman at ease, Magnus had pointed to the pallet and motioned for her to lie upon it. He pointed at a corner and then thumbed his chest: he would sleep there.

After Kinga had settled herself nervously on the pallet, Magnus spread the red, yellow, and black striped blanket over her thinly clothed body to protect her from a slight chill in the night's air. Then, as he had promised, he retired to a far corner. Instead of sleeping, though, Magnus sat with his back against the wall, staring through the long, narrow window at the Caribbean sky blazing with stars.

Noticing how stiffly Kinga was lying on the pallet, Magnus knew that she was not sleeping. But, still, he did not bother her. It was not until he saw a star shooting across the twinkling sky that he raised his hand and pointing toward the heavens, he whispered, "Look!"

Bolting upward, Kinga stared at Magnus with alarm. Then seeing his finger pointing toward the window, she gasped at the sight of the starry night beyond.

Soon, Magnus and Kinga stood side by side in front of the window, watching the stars as they shimmered against the blackness. Seeing another falling star, Magnus pointed his hand for Kinga to follow its fiery trail. He chuckled at how she gasped at its magnificence. Then remembering how long she had been locked away from nature, kept shackled to a cruel existence in the Barracoon, he understood her awe at seeing an expanse of sky again.

Tapping Kinga on the shoulder, Magnus motioned for her to go to bed. He knew that her first day above the water line had been both exciting and terrifying for her. He had noticed in the harbor yard that afternoon what hatred Pra showed for Kinga. Magnus had seen the hurt in Kinga's eyes as she watched Pra talking with new intimacy to the other Ashantis, who now avoided her.

On that first night together, three nights ago, when Magnus had tried to force Kinga to get some rest, she had shaken her head and pulled him to stand beside her by the window. He did not know how long they had stayed there, staring at the stars, but he did remember that she had moved her warm body closer against him. At last, she was not frightened of him; she was slowly accepting him as at least a friend.

They had lain together that first night on the pallet, Kinga falling immediately to sleep in Magnus's arms, her intricate plaits pressed against his shoulder. Magnus counted each breath she took. She already seemed to be part of him. When he felt his manhood harden with a natural desire for her, he told himself to be patient, that if he truly respected this young woman, he could wait to consummate their love. Why chance some possible beauty in their future for a fleeting moment of lust?

Apart from his desires to build a friendship with Kinga before pursuing a sexual relationship, Magnus had also heard from Lolly Mumba what a depraved torture Abdee had subjected Kinga to, how Abdee had ordered Pra to sew golden wires through the tender lips of her womanhood—and adhered them together with molten alloy.

Magnus remembered Abdee refer fleetingly to something he had done to Kinga. Abdee had spoken of it on the same day he had given Magnus permission to pursue his friendship with the Ashanti woman. Magnus was glad now that Abdee had not explicitly told him about the golden wires or Magnus feared that he might have attacked Abdee, such a loss of temper would only have cancelled any future for Magnus with the only female for whom he felt a consuming love.

Lying again tonight alongside Kinga, the third night after Abdee had sailed for Martinique, Magnus knew that he had learned very little about her in the last three days. They spoke a patois of African and English with one another, and from those conversations Magnus understood that Kinga had been married to an Ashanti chieftain, that her husband had been killed in the same raid against their village in which she was taken as a slave. He quickly recognized her compassion for other black people and that she believed Pra was misleading her tribesmen with harmful superstitions and rebellious talks.

Above anything else, Magnus understood that Kinga was a human being starved for some show of kindness, desirous to feed herself on the simplicity of nature, to share warmth, ideas, the world. Magnus was willing to fulfil those wishes. He gladly controlled his sexual urges to mate with her. The mere thought of the pain caused by needles piercing her womanhood made even him—a man—wince. He had no desire to inflict more pain upon her until she was healed in both health and spirit.

And those were Magnus's thoughts on the third

night he shared a pallet with Kinga in a tower room of *Castelo Novo Mundo*. Like the previous two nights, he had slept little, lying awake to enjoy her nearness. He saw the sky lightening outside the window as the sun crept closer toward the far off horizon. Above the sound of the surf lapping against the castle's craggy base, he heard the crow of a cockerel cut the stillness. He was planning what he would do today—the fourth day—for Kinga, when the door to the room slowly opened. Magnus was wishfully plotting their future, not hearing the black people who crept into the room. He did not see Pra and his followers until they surrounded the pallet, pointing long guns and spears at him and Kinga.

*   *   *

Kinga had been dreaming about her husband, seeing him in her dream arguing with Pra. As usual, Pra shouted while her husband remained calm. Pra shouted louder and Kinga suddenly sat up from her pallet. But she did not know if she was still dreaming or not. She saw Pra. He was holding a spear to her husband. Then Pra shouted at Kinga—calling her Sabata Abadie—and she looked at her husband only to see that she had been sleeping with the black man with the kind eyes, the chieftain of *Castelo Novo Mundo* called . . . Magnus.

Tugging Kinga up from the pallet by her arm, Pra told her that he had come to take away this black man who was the consort of the white devils. That the black people now controlled this rock built in the middle of the river. Pra bragged that he now also had a consort. He had a white consort who knew how to sail the canoe driven by the wind. That his consort would soon be arriving back at this rock. That the Africans must punish this black consort of the white devil. That Kinga's life was only being spared because of her husband's position in the Ashanti tribe.

Then, pulling Kinga across the room, Pra shoved her down the spiral stairs, prodding her when she turned to see what the other blacks were doing to Magnus. Pra told her that she would soon see enough in the harbor yard, a sight which would remind her forever never to befriend a black traitor.

* * *

Wooden pegs had been driven into the harbor yard, and, after Magnus's legs and arms had been stretched and tied to the pegs by leather thongs, the clothes were ripped from his body and Pra began his tortures.

First, Pra slashed Magnus's brown skin with a thin silver blade until blood poured from the long gashes; the gashes first looked to Kinga like tribal tattoo marks but she turned her head away when she saw the blood begin to ooze from each elongated cut. And Pra opened each incision wider to make the blood pour more freely, running down Magnus's brown chest in rivulets of red.

Pra shouted for his men to make Kinga watch the torture. She had tried to use the red, yellow, and black striped blanket to cover her face but the guards ripped it from her hands and threw it to the dirt.

Next, Pra twisted wires around the roots of Magnus's testicles. Magnus's screams began to echo in the stone walls surrounding the harbor.

Looking frantically around the yard for someone to help Magnus, Kinga saw no kindness in any of the black faces. Even Lolly Mumba and the Ibo guards watched approvingly as Pra proceeded with this vindictive ritual. He had won them all.

Drawing six long silver needles from a cloth, Pra began to insert them into the bloody gashes he had made across Magnus's chest. Kinga tried to cover her ears when she heard Magnus cry. The needles were sinking into his open wounds. Pra gently tapped the head of each needle, alternating between them, pushing each point deeper and deeper into the bleeding flesh, pointing their long sharpness toward Magnus's heart and lungs.

Stopping momentarily, Pra raised himself from Magnus's writhing body and stared at Kinga. He boomed, "Sabata Abadiel"

Her breasts heaving, she glared at Pra's face welted with the tribal marks long ago healed into crooked seams.

Once having her full attention, Pra nodded at the two men standing nearest to Magnus. The men bent over Magnus's spread legs and they each took one end of the wire tied around his scrotum. They began to pull in opposite directions.

Again, hearing Magnus's screams turn into a painful wail, Kinga tried to wrench herself free from the guards.

And, again, Pra boomed, "Sabata Abadiel"

She glared at him with hatred. She spit at him. She threw back her head and screamed, *"M-fo!"*

Smiling, Pra turned to Magnus. And slowly raising his right leg, the Ashanti tribesman lowered the calloused pinkness of his foot, using it to press the needles deeper into the area around Magnus's heart.

Dizziness began to overtake Kinga. She slumped forward, hearing Pra booming "Sabata Abadie" as the guards let her collapse onto the dirt of the harbor yard.

20

"... AND THE LORD TAKETH AWAY!"

"We thought you were dead," Captain Pennington announced to Richard Abdee as he stood next to a chair which had been brought for Abdee to the quarterdeck of the *Petit Jour*. Abdee was too weak to stand, too weary to tell Pennington to stop his windy explanations about how he and the crew had found him on the previous night crawling from the rubble of the manor house at *Côte Rouge*.

Despite the dullness in his brain, Abdee noticed that Pennington was in an unnaturally good humor. Pennington looked toward the bulky outline of *Castelo Novo Mundo* in the distance and continued with an obvious smugness to his voice, "We saw the first explosion and thought, by Jove, another ship was jolly well astern. Some of us even turned to look. Then—with a quick boom! boom! boom!—we heard three more roars. We looked toward the house again and saw those cannons blasting the sea wall. By then, the house was bursting with flame and smoke. We knew we'd better investigate.

"Mad! You were quite raving mad, Abdee. We found you beyond the smouldering shambles of some columned porch there. You were right screaming mad, you were. Ranting about going back into the house to fetch some treasures. You kept jabbering about taxes!"

Pulling at his ginger whiskers, chuckling, Pennington said, "Taxes! Screaming about taxes at a time like that! You were in no condition—mentally or physically, Abdee—to go anywhere.

"The only rushing being done there was by plantation darkies. We saw black folks running everywhere. To the hills. To the woods. Down the road. Across the fields. Up the slopes. The whole slave quarters scattered—and good, I say. Good! That frog, Saint-Barbot, he died in the fire. And it was good those poor folk finally got out of there.

"You should be thankful, Abdee, that I was at hand. That the Lord sent me in the nick of time!"

Gripping the arms of the chair, Abdee roared, "The Lord? A pox on your Lord! I *told* you to be there, you bloody fool! If you remember, I also warned you to anchor to the south of *Côte Rouge*. I *told* you about those bloody cannons!"

Repositioning his hands behind his back, Pennington answered with calm assurance, "Blaspheming the Lord won't serve your recuperation Mister Abdee. Your legs were burned. Your arm cut up. You've been unconscious the whole night and half the morning. You're a sick man."

Abdee muttered, "Unconscious, hell! I was sleeping, you damned ass." Then looking beyond the prow, Abdee suddenly forgot about Pennington and his girlish fondness for exaggeration. He stared with disbelief at the castle as the wind carried the *Petit Jour* closer toward it. Abdee heard the sailors behind him rolling the foresails, slackening the spars. They were preparing for entry into *Castelo Novo Mundo* but the gate had not been raised. He ranted, "Damn that Magnus! Hasn't he kept a lookout for us?"

Ignoring Abdee's temper, Pennington withdrew a brass plated spyglass from his belt. He slowly opened it and raised it to his eye. He smiled as he studied the castle. Then, lowering the spyglass, Pennington stood on the heaving deck and looked at the castle with his naked eye. He was still smiling.

Snatching the spyglass from Pennington's hand, Abdee slowly steadied himself on the railing, ignoring the pain in both his legs. He moved toward Pennington and looked through the lens himself. He carefully studied the sea at the castle's base, where the hewn stones joined the bedrock. He discerned a movement, soon seeing the shapes of people. Black people. Black people armed with long guns and spears. They were not welcoming him.

Lowering the spyglass, he muttered, "Bastards."

Turning, summoning what little physical strength he had, trying to ignore the arm wound beginning to bleed again, Abdee shouted, "Fire on them! Use the swivel cannons! Blast them into the sea!"

Not moving, Pennington asked, "Fire? Fire on your own people, Mister Abdee?" He shook his head.

"I said fire!"

Pennington still did not move. He firmly stated, "I will not fire on any living creature."

Then, reaching for his pistol to force Pennington to follow his order, Abdee found that he had been disarmed. He had no pistol. No blade. Not even a whip at hand.

Turning from Pennington's smirking face, Abdee

hobbled to look toward the main deck. The crew was beginning to gather there. Abdee saw a strange soberness to the men's faces. Even Tewes was a different person now.

Stepping alongside Abdee, Pennington shouted, "Lower a long boat."

"A long boat?" Abdee demanded. "Where in the hell are you going in a long boat?"

"Me? I'm not going anywhere, Mister Abdee. *You* are. Oarsmen are going to row you to meet your . . . people. You are going to listen to their terms. *I* now give the orders aboard the *Petit Jour*."

Abdee gasped at him.

Raising his chin, Pennington said, "It's a recorded fact of marine history, as in all life itself, Mister Abdee, that men follow orders from superiors who feed and clothe them. Let me remind you, Mister Abdee, that you failed to pay your men their rightful wages since well before we sailed for New Orleans."

Abdee's words were not a question. He said, "You've called a mutiny."

Nodding toward the long boat now ready to splash down into the sea, Pennington said, "Mutiny isn't half of it, Mister Abdee. Now get into that boat. Go see for yourself what Pra has to tell you."

"*Pra?*"

Pennington nodded. "Pra. He's one of the Africans you saw through the spyglass standing outside the walls. Pra is waiting there to speak to you. I recognized some time ago he has a natural talent for leadership. The *Petit Jour* will be taking Pra and his followers to Santo Domingo."

Abdee stared at Pennington in disbelief.

Pennington continued, "Santo Domingo has a colony of blacks. They live a free life there. I have already agreed to take Pra and his people to Santo

Domingo. From there, the *Petit Jour* will sail independently. This crew has agreed to share the profits of a commercial venture until, perhaps, they find more advantageous employment elsewhere. Or—" He looked soberly at Abdee. "—if our commercial venture does not prove successful, Mister Abdee, we shall sell the *Petit Jour* and divide the sum between us in fair and just shares . . . a small recompense for these good men's long hours of duty to a disreputable man such as yourself."

Completely sober now, Pennington concluded, "Mister Abdee, I sincerely urge you to take advantage of what the Lord is offering you. The Lord Almighty is often impatient with sinners such as yourself who refuse to accept his graces. It is then that the Lord deems it necessary to take everything away. Everything, Mister Abdee. So, I advise you to get into that boat or you'll have to swim to your accursed . . . *Castelo Novo Mundo!*" Pennington spat out the words as if they were poison on his tongue.

*   *   *

Pra stood on the crags at the base of *Castelo Novo Mundo*, a few of his black followers crowded behind him, their bare feet clinging to the sharp stones like the talons of sea birds.

As the sailors rowed the long boat from the *Petit Jour*, the oars neatly slicing the water in unison, Abdee slouched in the prow. Pra called in monosyllabic words to the approaching boat, verifying the facts which Captain Pennington had told Abdee on the ship's quarterdeck.

Pra turned from the lapping waves and grabbed a black woman from the narrow ledge of rocks between the castle walls and the sea. The woman was Kinga. Pulling her to stand, Pra shoved her toward the

African men standing alongside him. He next bent to the rocks and lifted a limp, blood-smeared body of a man. He faced the long boat, holding out the dead body for Abdee to see that it was Magnus before tossing him into the surf with a splashing thud.

The sound of chains soon began to clank and grind inside the wall; the gate slowly lifted and, as the sailors proceeded to row Abdee into the harbor, Pra and his followers scrambled along the craggy base. They dragged Kinga with them as they agilely moved over the narrow footpath edging the entrance into the harbor.

Black people began to emerge from behind doors and wooden gates, gathering in the dirt yard. They stared at Abdee's slouched figure in the prow of the boat. They spoke among themselves in African, mostly in Ashanti and Ibo dialects, even those men, women, and children who had once used their master's tongue. And then, as the *Petit Jour* creaked and heaved under the raised portcullis, the black people scurried to gather the bundles and animals they were taking with them and they crowded toward the ship to leave *Castelo Novo Mundo*.

* * *

Abdee lay on the dirt in the empty harbor yard, his back propped against a stone wall. He stared blankly through the gate left open after the *Petit Jour* had sailed from the harbor, set on its northwesterly course to Santo Domingo.

Dirty sons-of bitches, he muttered.

Having found a red, yellow, and black striped blanket crumpled in a far corner of the harbor yard, Abdee now pulled it around his shivering body, mumbling to himself that he was surprised that the Africans had not taken the blanket, too.

They took everything else. Every hen, pig, rabbit they could find. Those bastards cleared out this place worse than that Frenchman.

Abdee had not touched food in forty-eight hours. Deciding now to search the castle for scraps, he tried to raise himself up from the ground but fell back when a pain shot through both his legs.

Flesh burns heal, he convinced himself, resettling himself against the wall.

Forcing himself to forget about food, he pulled the blanket further around his shoulders. Although he felt as if the evening air was becoming rapidly cooler, he knew that he might have to wait here much longer than tonight—and tomorrow night—for the *Casa d' Oro* to arrive back from Africa.

Ignatio Soto, that cunning old Cuban fox, he'll get here with that new load of blacks. I can count on that. Half of them are mine, too.

Then remembering the gold which Soto had given him for security, the money which Abdee had spent to buy the mortgage on *Côte Rouge*, he took another sigh. He thought how he might have to take less than a fifty percent cut of the slave cargo.

Who knows? Maybe that crooked Cuban won't even give me half. Maybe he won't even come back here at all. Or maybe he'll get back and refuse to give me anything . . . the hell with it! I'll think of something.

His eyelids becoming heavy now, Abdee decided to sleep for a while. But as his chin rested against his shoulder, he blinked, half looking at the scarlet light of the sinking sun shimmering on the Caribbean beyond the open gate.

Suddenly, he raised his head with a jerk. He saw something bobbing in the surf. He could not tell at first what he was seeing out there but . . . *what is it?*

Realizing with a start that he was looking at a bloated corpse, that he was seeing Magnus's body floating past the gate, Abdee felt his empty stomach heave. He wretched. His gags were empty, painful.

Turning sideways, gasping to fill his lungs with air, he stared at the filth strewn yard to divert his mind. He saw plank doors hanging from their leather hinges. The posterns led to steps strewn with manure and straw. He saw that the Africans had even ripped off the new iron grille which he and Magnus had built to the entrance of the Barracoon.

What the hell didn't they take? The more he studied the harbor yard, though, the better he felt. He soon was smiling to himself. He remembered when he had first seen this place. He had been the master of Dragonard Plantation on St. Kitts at the time. Naomi was living with him. He had bought this place as a depot for shipping sugar from all these islands to mills in England. He had not even thought of using it as a slave station at that time. He had been rich then. Powerful . . .

When a black rebellion destroyed Dragonard Plantation, though, he had to move here. This was the only place then he had to go. And Naomi?

He forced himself again to forget about Naomi. She was dead. He did not want to have any dreams that she had possibly survived. That she was still alive somewhere in the world.

Trying to concentrate on how he had first found this island, the small price he had paid a Portuguese merchant in Curacao for it, Abdee found his spirit strengthening. He remembered how he had rallied his ambitions before. He knew that he could do it all over again.

Coughing, Abdee held his chest with both arms as he bent forward, a bloody spittle streaming from his mouth, the cough cutting across his chest, his forearm starting to bleed again from the sword wound.

Damn that fat Cuban, he muttered. *Why doesn't he get here!*

Leaning his head back against the stone wall, wishing that he at least had a bottle of black rum to warm his belly, Abdee looked up at the castellated walls surrounding the harbor yard. He admitted to himself that the place looked doomed and Godforsaken.

The yellow and red bile was now beginning to stream from his mouth, dribbling over the stubble on his chin. But he kept pushing his thoughts toward the future, trying to make some kind of plan as he looked at the abandoned tower rooms, the empty windows, the lifeless walls—blankly gazing upwards at the cold and lonely enclosure of . . . *Dragonard Rising.*

ABOUT THE AUTHOR

The author was born over thirty years ago on the Leeward Island of Nevis. The seventh generation of an English colonial family, he was the first to break away from plantation life. After attending preparatory school in Rhode Island, he studied on the Continent. Then, traveling extensively in Africa and the Far East, he returned home when he first came up with the idea for the Dragonard saga, which was published under his pseudonym, RUPERT GILCHRIST. He now lives in Montserrat in a seventeenth-century captain's house, which he has faithfully restored himself. His hobbies include horses, skin-diving, collecting African artifacts and tuning the engine of his Lamborghini. He has also written under his real name.